Just on the ~~other~~ r, his rifle out and aimed where Slocum would have appeared if he hadn't gotten suspicious.

"Looking for me?" Slocum asked.

The rustler jerked around, startled. Before he could train his rifle on Slocum, he caught a bullet in the gut. The rustler staggered and fell to his knees, but he was tougher than he looked. He fought to bring the rifle up and shoot Slocum. Slocum waited a moment and finally saw that the man was going to succeed through either sheer determination or outright meanness. It didn't matter which. Slocum took an easy shot. The rustler sighed and collapsed, dead.

DON'T MISS THESE
ALL-ACTION WESTERN SERIES
FROM THE BERKLEY PUBLISHING GROUP

THE GUNSMITH by J. R. Roberts
Clint Adams was a legend among lawmen, outlaws, and ladies. They called him . . . the Gunsmith.

LONGARM by Tabor Evans
The popular long-running series about Deputy U.S. Marshal Long—his life, his loves, his fight for justice.

SLOCUM by Jake Logan
Today's longest-running action Western. John Slocum rides a deadly trail of hot blood and cold steel.

BUSHWHACKERS by B. J. Lanagan
An action-packed series by the creators of Longarm! The rousing adventures of the most brutal gang of cutthroats ever assembled—Quantrill's Raiders.

DIAMONDBACK by Guy Brewer
Dex Yancey is Diamondback, a Southern gentleman turned con man when his brother cheats him out of the family fortune. Ladies love him. Gamblers hate him. But nobody pulls one over on Dex . . .

WILDGUN by Jack Hanson
The blazing adventures of mountain man Will Barlow—from the creators of Longarm!

TEXAS TRACKER by Tom Calhoun
Meet J.T. Law: the most relentless—and dangerous—man-hunter in all Texas. Where sheriffs and posses fail, he's the best man to bring in the most vicious outlaws—for a price.

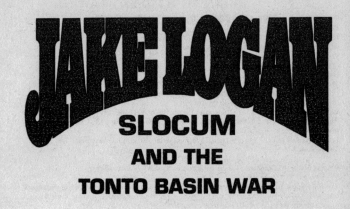

JAKE LOGAN

SLOCUM
AND THE
TONTO BASIN WAR

JOVE BOOKS, NEW YORK

THE BERKLEY PUBLISHING GROUP
Published by the Penguin Group
Penguin Group (USA) Inc.
375 Hudson Street, New York, New York 10014, USA
Penguin Group (Canada), 90 Eglinton Avenue East, Suite 700, Toronto, Ontario M4P 2Y3, Canada
(a division of Pearson Penguin Canada Inc.)
Penguin Books Ltd., 80 Strand, London WC2R 0RL, England
Penguin Group Ireland, 25 St. Stephen's Green, Dublin 2, Ireland (a division of Penguin Books Ltd.)
Penguin Group (Australia), 250 Camberwell Road, Camberwell, Victoria 3124, Australia
(a division of Pearson Australia Group Pty. Ltd.)
Penguin Books India Pvt. Ltd., 11 Community Centre, Panchsheel Park, New Delhi—110 017, India
Penguin Group (NZ), Cnr. Airborne and Rosedale Roads, Albany, Auckland 1310, New Zealand
(a division of Pearson New Zealand Ltd.)
Penguin Books (South Africa) (Pty.) Ltd., 24 Sturdee Avenue, Rosebank, Johannesburg 2196,
South Africa

Penguin Books Ltd., Registered Offices: 80 Strand, London WC2R 0RL, England

SLOCUM AND THE TONTO BASIN WAR

A Jove Book / published by arrangement with the author

PRINTING HISTORY
Jove edition / January 2007

ISBN: 978-0-515-14242-6

JOVE®
Jove Books are published by The Berkley Publishing Group,
a division of Penguin Group (USA) Inc.,
375 Hudson Street, New York, New York 10014.
JOVE is a registered trademark of Penguin Group (USA) Inc.
The "J" design is a trademark belonging to Penguin Group (USA) Inc.

PRINTED IN THE UNITED STATES OF AMERICA

10   9   8   7   6   5   4   3   2   1

1

Lies. Nothing but lies everywhere John Slocum looked. The billowing white clouds swung across the burning hot Arizona sun, promising rain and not delivering a drop. More than once as he rode north from Tombstone, he had seen small oases where water had to pool. It hadn't. The Arizona desert was almost impossible to cross, and it wore heavily on Slocum and his horse, to the point where they traveled only at night. Even then, keeping enough water on his chapped lips proved damned near impossible. He had to roll a small stone around in his mouth to even pretend he had tasted water, and this old Indian trick was beginning to fail. There simply wasn't spit left in his body.

"Lies, all lies," Slocum grumbled as he rode. He shook his head and caused a small cascade of dust to fall all around him off his wide-brimmed hat. He used his bandanna to wipe away the constant river of sweat on his forehead, cleared his vision and stared ahead into the heat-hazy distance. Mountains. Cool, tree-covered mountains. Or more lies? He knew how distances in the desert were deceiving, especially to a man who hankered after water like he did now.

Slocum was a betting man, but he wouldn't risk his life

on finding water anytime soon. That kept his pace slow and deliberate, hiding from the sun and only exerting himself until his horse began to flag, then resting the remainder of the night.

For the first few nights, when he had made only a few scant miles of progress, he had worried about men who might be dogging his footsteps. After a week, he knew that the men he had crossed in Tombstone weren't anywhere near as dumb as he had thought. They had stayed in town and let him ride into the desert to die.

Slocum settled his bandanna around his neck again and kept riding slowly toward the mountains. The sun had been up for almost an hour and he ought to find a hidey hole and some shade.

A feathery-leafed mesquite bush offered as much shade as anything he was likely to find out here, and even had sprouted bean pods his horse could eat. He saw nothing else, not even the towering saguaros riddled with owl nests and flights of annoying insects, so he pushed on in spite of the rapidly rising heat.

Within a half hour he wondered if he had made a fatal mistake. After forty-five minutes he was saved. He was riding, drifting and hardly paying any attention to where his horse headed when the mare tossed her head and trotted due west instead of northerly to the Sierra Anchas mountains.

"Whoa, where you going?" The sudden change had brought Slocum out of his deadly lethargy. Another few minutes and he would have fallen from horseback. If that had happened, his bones would have been picked clean by the vultures already circling above, and what the carrion eaters left would have bleached over the next twenty years.

"Water," he croaked out. His eyes squinted against the sun to be certain a mirage wasn't giving him false hope. Then he realized that he might hallucinate, but his horse's nose would lead her to water every time. No mirage could produce the eagerness he felt now. Giving the mare her head, he reached the small pool of water within minutes and didn't bother dismounting. He simply fell into the pool. It was shallow, muddy and the sweetest water he had ever tasted.

Flopping around in the foot-deep water revived him. He drank slowly until he was strong enough to stand and shake off the water like a wet dog might. Then he dragged the mare back to keep her from bloating.

"More soon, I promise," he said to the horse. A big brown accusing eye turned toward him. He patted the horse and looked around for forage. A few weeds grew nearby. He let the mare crop at them before permitting another long drink from the pool. Then Slocum filled his canteen and lounged back in the shade of a scrub oak sprouting up out of the impossibly rocky landscape. He had gotten close enough to the mountains to find a spring.

He had taken the crookedest gamblers in Tombstone for a small fortune, dared the desert and had beaten it, too. He felt mighty pleased with himself as he drifted off to sleep in the hot morning sun.

Slocum sat up fast, his hand going to the Colt Navy slung in its cross-draw holster when he heard gunfire. The leather had gotten wet during his plunge into the pool and then dried. The six-shooter came out slower than usual. Slocum relaxed, knowing he had to clean the precision weapon before firing it. The Colt didn't cotton much to getting dunked in water, but that didn't take away from the renewed flurry of gunshots echoing across the desert.

Someone was in a passel of trouble. Whether it was anything he should get involved with had to be decided. Working quickly, Slocum stripped the six-gun down, wiped off the mechanism with his shirttail and wished he had time to properly oil it before using it. The gunfire hadn't died down, as he had hoped. If anything, it grew more intense.

"Come on, one last drink, and we hit the trail," Slocum said to his mare. He led the horse to the pool and let her drink more. He dropped to his knee and scooped up a drink for himself, then vaulted into the saddle. From this added elevation he could see more clearly the direction of the gunfire.

Luck, if he could call it that, rode with him again. The shots came from the north, toward the Sierra Anchas, where he had sought refuge from the heat. Since he was going that way no matter what he found, he urged his horse forward at a walk. His instincts cried out for him to rush ahead, but that would be foolish. Blundering into the middle of a range war was the surest way of getting shot by both sides.

Fifteen minutes later, Slocum followed a deep-cut arroyo and then drew rein. He dismounted, tethered the horse to a greasewood and advanced on foot until he came up behind a pair of Apache braves all decked out for the warpath. Slocum sank down behind the arroyo bank and tried to remember even a snippet of rumor that the Apaches were kicking up a fuss. In this part of Arizona there were any number of tribes. Some had been relocated to reservations. The Warm Springs Apaches from New Mexico spent most of their time leaving the reservation, raiding and hiding out in Mexico, causing nothing but headaches for the cavalry. But these braves weren't Warm Springs. Slocum had never seen this particular variety of war paint before but thought it might be Tonto Apache.

Not that it mattered. He was as dead from a Tonto bullet as he would be from a Warm Springs or Mescalero. He was ready to sneak back to his horse and avoid the skirmish when he heard a loud voice call out, "We'll surrender if you promise not to kill us. Take the beeves but let us keep our scalps!"

Slocum wondered what sort of fool tried to dicker with the Indians like that. If the Apaches thought they had the rancher and whatever cowboys rode with him in a box, they would never let him go free.

Cursing under his breath, Slocum circled the two braves and worked his way to the top of a rocky hill, where he got a better idea of how desperate the rancher's situation was. The rancher had a dozen head of cattle, all lowing in fright and threatening to stampede as the Indians kept up a ragged, deadly fire. Slocum did a quick count. Three wranglers herded a dozen cattle and were surrounded by more than twenty Apache braves. The odds were wildly skewed in favor of the Indians. Chances were mighty good they would have steaks for dinner while the cowboys would be buzzard bait.

"Don't, Papa, don't," came a voice that froze Slocum in his tracks. He wiggled back and studied the trio in the draw. Two men were big, burly and wore their hats pulled down low to keep the sun out of their eyes. The third was smaller and had pushed back a Stetson to let flowing auburn hair blow away from her face.

Slocum cursed a blue streak. If it had been three cowboys, he might have left them to their fate. But he couldn't slip away and let the Apaches get their filthy hands on a woman. The men would die. The woman would suffer for years.

Slocum couldn't hear the rest of the discussion between the woman and her father because gunfire drowned out the words. As he watched, he saw an Apache warrior wiggling closer. The Indian drew a bead on one of the three. Slocum rolled to his side, aimed and fired in a smooth motion. His first shot kicked up dust into the brave's face. The Indian recoiled, startled and not knowing what direction the bullet had come from. Slocum didn't give him time to find out and warn the others in the war party. His second shot caught the Apache squarely in the side of the head. The man fell facedown, dead before he realized he had been shot.

Rolling back to his belly and keeping his head down, Slocum worried that the others in the war party would have seen him. He poked his head up and looked around. He need not have worried. There was too much commotion for them to notice a couple shots amid the flurry that came from the two cowboys and the woman. Slocum noted with approval how good a marksman the woman was. She never hurried her shots, always squeezed back and usually hit— or at least came close—to her living targets.

Still, the tide was against the trio. Slocum tried to see how he could help them more than he already had. There wasn't any way in hell. Too many Indians, too few guns pointing back at them. Even if Slocum crept about and back-shot as many Apaches as he could, he didn't have enough ammo to make a difference. Getting himself captured, or more likely killed, helped no one.

"This isn't your fight," Slocum muttered to himself, even as he knew he was lying. He didn't know these people or how they had allowed themselves to get trapped by the war party, but he wasn't going to let them be captured and butchered.

He got a better look at the woman as she frantically pumped at the lever of her rifle. It had come up empty. The cowboy beside her soon ran dry, too, leaving only her father with ammunition.

"We surrender!" the man called, waving his rifle over his head. "Don't kill us. We got kin who can ransom us!"

Slocum nodded approval. This would buy them some time. Swapping hostages for cattle, horses or weapons was a time-honored tradition of most tribes. He didn't doubt the prospect of getting a few more horses for his remuda appealed to the war chief leading the Tontos.

All the chief had to do was hold his braves in check. From the fierce expressions on the faces Slocum could see, that might not be easy. Slocum guessed the Indians had recently gone off the reservation, and these three might be their first victims. The sight of so many cattle on the hoof had to appeal to the Indians, as well, after the maggoty food they were likely given on the reservation.

The war chief, a strongly built man, tall for an Apache, stood and let out a bloodcurdling ululation that carried over the desert and halfway into the hills beyond. Slocum watched the two cowboys and the woman throw down their rifles and put their hands high into the air. Then the braves rushed them, roughing them up. It took all his self-control for Slocum not to empty his pistol at the Apaches groping the woman. He had to admire her courage, though. She stared straight ahead and tried not to let it show that the way they touched her—and where—bothered her. Slocum considered waving, trying to attract her attention and letting her know he would be rescuing her soon. Good sense prevailed. If she saw him, she might react.

Or the Apaches might spot him. Slocum slipped back down the stony hillside and found a deep ravine to shield him from sight. He ran silently back to his horse and mounted. It wouldn't take the Indians long to decide what they were going to do with their captives. The men might be killed outright and the woman forced into slavery. Or all three might be taken to the war camp for ransoming.

Slocum started to ride closer, then held back. The Apaches would leave a trail any greenhorn could follow, because they thought they were alone—and they had just scored a major victory. They would drive the cattle to their camp, even if they killed the men. That was a trail Slocum knew could not be hidden.

Fuming at the necessary delay, worrying that inaction now might mean three deaths, Slocum dismounted and found a patch of shade against a particularly tall arroyo bank. He sat and worked on his six-shooter, taking his repair kit from his saddlebags and giving the weapon a thorough cleaning and oiling. He had been lucky that it had fired when he had needed it. The next time he had to depend on skill rather than luck, because he would be trying to snatch three prisoners out from under the noses of two dozen alert Apaches on the warpath.

He tried to nap but kept jerking upright at every sound, no matter how small. When twilight danced through the arroyos and a brisk wind began blowing, he knew it was time to get on the trail. The Indians could be miles away by now, but Slocum doubted it. From what he had seen of the fight, the Apaches hadn't ambushed the drovers. Rather, the cattle had been driven past the Indians, who probably had no idea anyone was nearby. If the Apaches had ambushed the trio, they would have died within seconds.

Slocum found the ravine where the cattle had been bunched and saw the direction they had been driven. Although he might have missed it in the dusk, he saw no indication that the three with their cattle had been killed. He rode steadily, every sense straining for any hint he might be riding into the Apache camp. Less than an hour later, he sniffed and caught the hint of burning mesquite. The Apaches never ventured out at night, being afraid of rattlesnakes. Slocum thought it was probably more of a spiritual fear than actual, since he had seen Apaches grab the snakes with their bare hands and wave them about in broad daylight.

If they thought the snakes turned into evil spirits at night, Slocum wasn't going to argue with them. It made it easier getting into their camp. A few fearful sentries were all he need deal with.

When he had come within a few hundred yards of the Apache camp, he dismounted, got his bearings and advanced slowly. He had considered bringing his Winchester but decided his trusty knife sheathed in the top of his right boot was a better companion to the Colt Navy slung cross-draw style at his left hip. Stealth, not firepower, was going to free the captives.

If they were still alive.

As he had thought, the Apaches crowded around their fires. Three separate firepits blazed and crackled with dripping grease from the meat being roasted. Slocum's mouth watered at the delectable scent of cooking beef. It had been too long since he had eaten anything that hadn't come out of an airtight or been run down until it tasted gamy, no matter how he fixed it.

Slowly, he circled the campsite, finding only two guards. Both huddled under blankets, watching the fires and not the trails leading to the camp. He considered slitting the throats of the two inattentive guards but decided not to risk any outcry. Slocum moved past one and got closer to the largest fire, where the war chief sat cross-legged, gnawing on a bone that had recently been a cow rib.

The Apaches talked among themselves, but Slocum was more interested in catching a word or two of the lingo that he understood, to get an idea of what was being planned.

He figured out the young brave, hardly sixteen, next to the chief was his son. The young firebrand argued about killing. Slocum reckoned it had to be the captives. A cold lump formed in his belly when he realized the youngster was swaying his father.

Occasionally pointing with a rifle barrel in the direction of a large greasewood told Slocum where the trio was tied up. But getting to them would require a considerable amount of retracing his steps, circling and coming up on them. He didn't have the luxury of time. Not with the young brave beginning to shout and wave his rifle around wildly.

Slocum wondered what would happen if he killed the chief and a couple of the nastier-looking braves with him, but then he gave up the idea entirely. It would throw the band into confusion for a few seconds, but they were used to seeing their leaders killed in battle. Before every foray, the warriors elected a new war chief. One brave might be chief for years because of his expertise and bloodthirstiness, but he could be replaced the instant he showed any sign of flagging.

The youngster jumped to his feet and began dancing around. Slocum didn't recognize the particular dance. It wasn't a victory dance or a war dance, but it might have been something to do with slaughtering the bound captives. The other braves began to chant with the young brave's quick-moving feet, to show their approval. Slocum was more interested in the chief's expression.

While not pleased at having his authority usurped like this—he might have wanted to do as the rancher said and ransom the three—there was also a hint of pride. His son would be a great warrior one day, taking his place at the head of a war party.

Slocum hardly considered what he was doing. All eyes were on the dancing, gyrating brave when he stood, drew his knife and walked to the fire. If Slocum had run or tried to creep closer, he would have been spotted immediately. As it was, he blended in—for a few precious seconds.

Moving like a striking snake, Slocum grabbed the dancing youth by his hair and jerked hard, pulling his head back and exposing his throat. The sharp edge of the thick-bladed knife pressed into the brave's Adam's apple just hard enough to draw a thin red line.

"Don't do anything dumb," Slocum cautioned the chief, "unless you want your boy to die."

"He is a brave," the chief said, eyes wide with surprise. "He will be honored for dying in battle!"

"Some honor, letting a white-eyes walk into your camp and put a knife to your boy's throat." Slocum jerked harder on the handful of greasy hair when the young man tried to wiggle free. Spinning him around, Slocum put the brave between himself and three Apaches who had come up behind him.

"We got to do this quick," Slocum said. "We can all win, if you agree. You want your son killed?"

That Slocum knew whom he had captured so easily shocked the chief again.

"We can dicker. No time to pass around a pipe and think on it. You let go the three you captured this morning. On their horses. When you do that, I let your son go."

"I will kill you!" The youth struggled and got his chin down far enough so he could speak. Slocum put a knee into the boy's back to keep him from getting away or speaking again.

"I'm part of the deal. The three ranchers and me. We ride out of here, you get your boy back alive."

"Why should I trust you?"

"You speak mighty good English," Slocum said. "How's that?"

"I was taught in mission school," the chief said with more than a touch of bitterness. "I left our prison and killed them all."

"So much for the benefits of a good education," Slocum said. "But you have your honor to think about. You wouldn't break a deal, not if you swear a blood oath."

"No."

Slocum pulled the chief's son around again so the firelight reflected off the shiny silver blade. He pressed a bit more and drew more blood. Nothing serious. All he needed to do was sever one of the arteries pulsing hard in the youth's neck to kill him. But Slocum knew his own life would be over before the brave hit the ground.

"Time's running out. You swear to let us go, and I'll swear to let your son go."

"White men lie," the Apache spat out.

"I don't." Slocum spoke with such sincerity that the chief looked at him for the first time as if this deal might be done.

"Get the three," the chief ordered. A pair of braves rushed off and brought the trio back.

The cowboy had been shot in both arms, which hung limp at his sides. In a fight, he would be useless unless he could bite the Apaches, but from his fierce look he just might do that. The older man, the one the young woman had called her pa, looked leathery and tough enough to get through any scrape. His daughter again caught Slocum's attention. She looked frightened, but not to the point of being paralyzed. She was more than passing pretty and would be even better looking cleaned up. Right now sweat, dirt and blood marred her good looks. Her long auburn hair had fallen from under her Stetson and flopped about in greasy ropes.

"I've traded the chief his son's life for ours," Slocum said before the drover could say a word. Slocum didn't want a long, drawn out discussion.

"Who're you?" the rancher asked. "I'm Tewksbury. John Tewksbury. This is my daughter Lydia and that there's Caleb."

"Bring their horses," Slocum ordered the chief. "Now!"

"How are you going to get away?" Lydia asked. "If you—"

"The chief speaks better English than most trail hands," Slocum said, cutting her off. "Reckon he thinks quicker than most, too."

"Oh, I see," she said, and Slocum believed her. She was quick on the uptake and realized any discussion now only fed the chief's anger.

"Get on and ride back to where you came from," Slocum ordered them when three horses were led to the fireside.

"My cattle. I'm not leavin' a dozen strays with this damn cattle rustlin' varmint!" Tewksbury's outrage was ominous.

"Then you stay and argue the point with him. Caleb and your daughter can get the hell out of here with their scalps still where they ought to be."

The drover took in a deep breath, then silently swung into the saddle with the grace of a man twenty years younger.

"Lydia has a point. What about you?"

"I'll get by," Slocum said, already backing away. "You ride."

"We're in the Tonto Basin. The Circle T."

"Ride," Slocum said harshly. He waited for the three to vanish into the night, then began backing away toward where he had tethered his horse.

"You let him go. Now!"

"You stay where you are," Slocum warned. "I give you my blood oath I won't hurt him unless you try to stop me." Slocum pricked the skin on his left hand and held it up, showing the sluggish red drop flowing down his palm. He continued to retreat until he came to where his horse waited nervously.

Slocum kicked out and drove his boot into the back of the young brave's knee, driving him to the ground. Swinging hard, he smashed the butt end of the heavy knife into the back of the Apache's head. He only stunned him, but that was good enough.

With a jump, Slocum mounted and turned his horse's face into the night. Behind, he heard the Apaches' angry cries. Bullets tore through the darkness after him, but he had ridden far enough to be out of range.

He thought about riding due west and getting the hell away from the Tonto Basin, which seemed to be in an uproar, but the thought of Lydia kept coming back to slow him. He hadn't rescued her, Caleb and John Tewksbury for a reward, but the thought of what she might give eventually caused him to swing from his westward route to a more northerly one.

It wouldn't hurt to see what the Circle T had to offer.

2

Apaches didn't ride at night. These did. Slocum heard the pounding hooves of Indian ponies before he had gone a mile. Cursing, he doubled back, then worked with a bit of scrub brush to hide his tracks, then barely hid in time as the war party rode up. The Apaches yammered at one another, shouting their insults and telling the young buck at their lead how foolish he was. This did not deter the chief's son.

He pointed angrily in the direction Slocum had been riding and took off, letting the others follow his lead or not. Some lingered, muttering curses as they gentled their agitated horses, but all followed eventually. Whether they feared their war chief or the young man was leader enough to inspire them didn't matter much to Slocum. The Apaches had taken the bogus trail and given him a few minutes' head start. Slocum led his horse from the arroyo where he had taken refuge and listened as the pounding hoofbeats faded into the night. Resting his hand on his six-shooter, he wondered if he might not trail them and pick off the braves at the rear of the party one by one. It would serve the chief's son right to be the only one who returned from his ill-considered mission.

Slocum pushed that notion out of his head. Petting a grizzly bear was a dumb idea. Thinking he could go up against a dozen Apache warriors all by himself was even stupider. He walked his horse a spell, then mounted and kept to low-lying areas to keep from silhouetting himself against the night sky. Like all the Arizona nights since he had ridden from Tombstone, it was cloudless and the blanket of stars shone brightly enough to read a newspaper. That made tracking easier and presented problems trying to elude the Indians.

As he rode, a cold certainty came to Slocum. If the son had come after him with half the party, that meant the chief had lit out after Tewksbury, Lydia and Caleb with the rest of the warriors. Like him, the trio might think there was no reason to hurry and that the Apaches wouldn't track them until morning, if then.

Slocum wondered at how badly he had tweaked the Apache honor by walking into their camp the way he had. To venture out at night ran counter to strong superstitions. He shrugged it off. Hatred knew no bounds, even when it came to spitting in the eye of a rattler turned into some ghostlike spirit.

Slocum circled and hunted for the trail left by the Tewksbury party. He found it around midnight and shook his head in disbelief when he saw it.

"Damnation," he muttered. "I freed a pack of fools." He dismounted and ran his finger over the outline of a cow hoofprint cut into the hard, dry dirt. "Those sons of bitches went back and stole their own cattle from the Apaches. No wonder the chief got such a burr in his moccasins." His initial anger passed and he had to laugh ruefully. It took real balls to do what Tewksbury had. It was crazy, but it appealed to Slocum. After all, hadn't he waltzed into the Apache camp without so much as a howdy-do and held the chief's son hostage?

Slocum mounted, and rode with growing anticipation of a fight. The small herd's tracks became obscure as the Indians' horses kicked up the trail. The chance of Tewksbury out-legging the chief while driving a dozen head of cattle at night was so slim as to be nonexistent. Slocum heard the neighing of horses before he spotted two Apaches on the trail ahead.

Slocum kept riding, as if he were one of their party. He got between the pair, drew his six-gun and fired point-blank into the brave on his left. He only winged the man, who let out a yelp and returned fire. By then Slocum had put his spurs to his mare's flanks and bolted ahead. The two braves fired at each other until they worked out what was happening. Slocum slowed, turned and took careful aim with his rifle. First one, then the other Apache died. It would have been better if they had shot each other, but Slocum wasn't complaining. He was alive and they were both dead.

"Two down, ten to go. More or less," Slocum said. He hadn't gotten an accurate count of how many Apaches there had been. The chief's son had led a few—maybe half—but the uncertainty of knowing even one made this rescue even more dangerous.

Gunfire from ahead lent speed to Slocum's advance. Tewksbury had ridden into the narrow mouth of a canyon, either because he knew the country or because he had been forced this way by his pursuers. If the former, there would be a way out. If the latter, and Tewksbury's luck had run out, he was caught in a box canyon. Slocum had seen more than one of these promising canyons peter out quick. Usually, getting away amounted to nothing more than back-tracking and finding some other route. This time it meant life or death to the rancher, his daughter and cowhand.

Slocum remembered how Caleb's arms had been useless. That made riding difficult and fighting impossible. Reduced to only the rancher and his daughter, they stood no chance at all of surviving. Even if they had stolen more ammo from the Apache camp, they were outnumbered five or six to one.

More gunfire was accompanied by the frightened bawl-ing of the cattle not slaughtered for the Apaches' dinner. Slocum slowed when he saw a head bobbing along in front of him. The Apache had gone to ground, possibly to am-bush Tewksbury if he managed to get past the rest of the

Indians. That told Slocum the Apaches weren't familiar with this part of the country. Otherwise, they would have been more confident of their attack.

Waiting for a moment brought unwanted attention as he sat in the middle of the trail. The brave swung around and fired. His slug went wide, but it forced Slocum to take cover. He put the mare between him and the brave, then decided boldness had carried hours before. Why not now?

Grabbing the saddle horn, he urged his horse ahead as he pulled himself up. From the Indian's position, all he saw was a horse trotting along. When Slocum rode a few yards past, he dropped down, swung around and whipped out his six-shooter. He fanned the Colt and got off four fast shots that ended the warrior's life. Slocum had to run to catch his horse, and found himself being shot at from all sides. He raced straight ahead, deeper into the canyon, until he saw a few head of cattle milling about aimlessly, frightened by the gunfire and unsure where to stampede.

"Don't shoot, it's me, Slocum!" he called as he galloped ahead. No bullets sang out toward him, telling him Tewksbury either was the most trusting galoot in the world or had run out of ammo.

Slocum hit the ground, ran a few steps and then dropped beside the rancher.

"You got yourself into a real pickle," Slocum said. "That rifle got any bullets?" Slocum indicated the rifle Tewksbury had rested atop a boulder.

"We're all out of ammo. You have some with you?"

"Sure, I always carry a carton or two when I'm fighting Apache renegades fresh off the reservation," Slocum said sarcastically.

"There's no need to be snippy about it," said Lydia, coming up to kneel beside her father. "A simple yes or no would suffice."

"It was stupid of you to steal the cattle instead of high-tailing it back to your ranch," Slocum said. His eyes locked with Lydia's ginger-colored ones. "A simple yes will do for an answer."

"You—"

"Hush up, daughter," Tewksbury said. "This ain't gettin' us nowhere fast."

"For once, you got that right," Slocum said. He had given the place a once-over and confirmed that the Tewksburys had ridden smack into a box canyon. "You have any idea how to get out of this trap, other than back through the Apaches?"

"New territory for me. I'm more at home in the Tonto Basin north of here. We was only huntin' strays this side of the Sierra Anchas. No call to come this way otherwise."

"From the look of it, you'll have plenty of time to figure out the lay of the land here," Slocum said.

"What's that supposed to mean?" Lydia Tewksbury was getting madder at him by the minute.

"We'll all spend an eternity looking up from our graves," Slocum said. "If the Apaches care to bury us."

"That's no attitude to have. We can get out!"

"How?" asked Slocum, but an idea was coming to him.

"I . . . I don't know," the woman said contritely.

"I got rid of three of them on my way in," Slocum said. "You have any idea how many are left?"

"You killed three of them? But—" Lydia was silenced by her father.

"Don't rightly know, Slocum. Might be ten left."

"Ten and all led by the war chief. I gave his son and another ten or so braves the slip, but eventually the kid will come back, tail between his legs. That'll double the guns we're facing."

"There you go again, sounding pessimistic."

"Miss Tewksbury," Slocum said angrily, "it's not pessimistic. It's the plain truth."

"Pa," called Caleb. "I found a trail to the rim. It's real narrow, but we can walk up it."

"He's your son?" Slocum looked at the wounded drover. Caleb had stuffed both his hands into the front of his torn, bloody shirt to keep them from flopping around. Otherwise, he seemed unhurt by the run-in with the Apaches.

"He is," Tewksbury said, a grimness in his tone that worried Slocum. As unrealistic as his daughter was about them getting out alive, the father was turning this into a defeat before it happened.

"Then you'll want to save both of them," Slocum said. "I've got an idea. Drive the cattle back out of the canyon and see if that's good enough for the Apaches to let us be."

"Not my cattle! I won't give them up to those red-skinned thieves!"

"Then those 'red-skinned thieves' are going to take your scalp. Hers will look mighty good hanging next to yours," Slocum said brutally. This shocked Tewksbury into grudging acceptance.

"Do you think it'll work, Slocum?" asked Caleb. "They'll be happy with the cattle and not our lives, too?"

Slocum doubted it, but driving the beeves back toward the Indians would create a diversion they could use to their advantage.

"Take your sister to the trail and get your asses up it pronto," Slocum said. "Me and your pa will take care of things here." Slocum fetched his Winchester and handed it to the older man. He took a few minutes to reload his Colt Navy, but knew they were not going to hold off almost a dozen Apaches if the chief decided to attack. Slocum wondered what was going through the Apache's mind right about now. Rattlesnake spirits walked at night, but honor demanded he get the cattle back and kill those who had made him look foolish. Would he figure he was ahead by simply keeping the herd?

"I don't like givin' them redskins my cattle. It took me damn near a week to round up those strays."

"It'll only take the Apaches a few seconds to lift your scalps," Slocum said. He ducked when Tewksbury swung the rifle around and fired three times, as fast as he could work the lever action.

"Damn Indians," Tewksbury said, but Slocum heard the resignation in the man's voice.

"Help me stampede the cattle," Slocum said. It hardly

seemed like a decent stampede. He had been caught in real
stampedes where five thousand head of cattle had spooked
and begun an unstoppable run across the prairie. Some-
times the lead cattle could be turned, but other times all that
could be done was ride alongside the frightened herd and
wait for them to tire, hoping not too many got trampled.

Slocum worked his way forward as Tewksbury fired
methodically to keep the Indians at bay. He reached the
milling, frightened beeves and had no trouble hurrahing
them into a lumbering retreat down the canyon into the
Apaches. They kicked up a dust cloud that obscured
Slocum's return to where Tewksbury had run out of ammo.
The rancher held up the rifle, silently imploring Slocum
for more bullets. Slocum took the rifle from the rancher.
They had run through all the ammunition.

"Let's let them sort out what's happening," Slocum
said, "and get the hell out of here."

He vaulted into the saddle. Tewksbury grabbed the reins
of his horse and mounted. Together they made their way to
the rear of the canyon, where Caleb's horse grazed at a
patch of tough grama grass. Slocum dropped to the ground,
patted the mare's neck and hoped the Apaches treated her
well. The mare had been a steadfast companion through
some harsh country.

"You gonna stand there or you gonna come?" Tewksbury had already pulled his saddlebags from his horse and
slung them over his shoulder. Slocum quickly duplicated
that effort. It was bad enough letting the chief have his
horse and tack, but Slocum was damned if he was going to
lose what other gear he carried.

"Race you to the top," Slocum said. He began the steep
climb, hoping Caleb hadn't been wrong about this going
all the way to the rim. Once they got to the high ground,
they could use an old Apache trick against the Indians, if
they were foolish enough to follow up the trail. Rocks
rolled down required nothing but some effort and a little
sweat. No bullets. He followed Tewksbury and almost ran
into the man when the rancher stopped suddenly.

"What's wrong?" A thousand problems raced through Slocum's mind. The narrow trail might have broken off from the cliff face. A rock fall could block further progress. Or the trail might have petered out.

"Caleb," called Tewksbury. "Why are you comin' back down?"

"Lydia," the young man said. Caleb walked cautiously, unable to balance himself well on the narrow ledge without the use of his hands. "She never made it up. She with you?"

Slocum looked past Tewksbury. There was no way they could have passed her on this trail. His eyes locked with Tewksbury's.

"Where'd she go?" Slocum asked. "She couldn't have started up the path unless she fell off. We'd've heard that." He considered what else could have happened. He added, "Or seen her as she fell past us."

In spite of himself, he looked over the edge, a hundred feet down into darkness. If Lydia Tewksbury had fallen, he would never see her in the gloomy canyon bottom.

"Her horse, Pa. It's got to be her horse."

"What are you talking about?" Slocum demanded. "You saying it threw her?"

"It's been hers since it was a colt. She's more attached to it than she is to any human bein'," Tewksbury said. He heaved a sigh, turned and put his hand on Slocum's shoulder. "Let me by. I've got to fetch her before the Apaches catch her."

"You're sure she's still on the canyon floor?" Slocum glanced out in the canyon but couldn't see anything because of long shadows and deep crevices cutting into the walls on both sides.

"Got to be," Caleb said. Caleb chewed on his lower lip and looked as if he might launch himself through thin air to get to the bottom so he could go after his wayward sister, too. Blood was thicker than water, but this dry Arizona ground would soak it all up, no matter how thick, and never leave a trace behind.

"Get to the top. Get on back to your ranch and fetch some help," Slocum said. "I'll get her. If I can."

"This isn't your fight, Slocum. You've done more than we got any right to expect," Tewksbury said.

The rancher stared into Slocum's cold green eyes and took a half step back.

"You don't have to go after Lydia," Tewksbury said. "She's my responsibility."

"Don't give the Indians something more to celebrate," Slocum said. "Take care of your son. I'll see to Lydia." He swung around on the path and worked his way back down the slippery slope, kicking up small pebbles as he stumbled and slid to the bottom. His mare greeted him with a snort and a toss of the head.

"Where'd she go?" Slocum asked the horse, as if it might answer. The mare backed away from him, pawed the rocky ground and tossed her head again, toward the far side of the canyon. Slocum considered where Lydia might have gone, foolishly thinking she could hide from Apaches who were clever enough to count horses and know when one was missing. Lydia either didn't know or had ignored that Indians considered horses to be wealth, in the same way the white man thought of gold and silver.

He swung into the saddle and trotted to the far side of the narrow box canyon. He didn't have to follow Lydia's trail. There simply was nowhere for her to hide. Slocum drew rein and stared straight at her, where she hunkered down in a rocky crevice.

"How'd you find me?" she asked.

"The Indians will be coming. I'm not sure there's time to get all the way up to the rim, but we've got to try," Slocum said.

"I will not!"

"Mighty fine horse," Slocum said, "but it'll be lonesome when the Apaches kill you."

"They won't find me ..." Lydia's voice trailed off. Slocum had obviously had no trouble locating her. The Indians wouldn't, either.

"Is your horse worth your life?" he asked. "Or being a squaw the rest of your life?"

Lydia shuddered as his words sank in.

"It's my horse," she said weakly.

Slocum jumped to the ground and tugged at his horse to get the mare closer to the crevice. Lydia's horse neighed loudly.

"There's no time," he said. "The Indians are coming."

Lydia took Slocum by surprise. The last thing in the world he expected from her was to swing a rock and clip him on the side of the head. He jerked as he caught sight of the motion, but his reaction caused him to smash his head into the side of the cliff, stunning him. In a flash Lydia pushed past, jumped into the saddle and started out of the canyon, following the sheer wall in hope of eluding the eager Apaches who whooped and hollered as they raced closer.

Slocum shook off the effect of the blow to his head, but he was wobbly. He had started to go after the woman when he saw a brave riding toward her. There wasn't any way Lydia Tewksbury could avoid being caught by the Indians.

3

Slocum reached for his rifle to take the Indian brave off his horse before he reached Lydia Tewksbury, but his hand groped and found only emptiness. He remembered he had lent the rifle to the woman's father and had abandoned it when its magazine came up empty. Not being able to fight at a reasonable distance, Slocum put his heels to his mare's flanks. The horse bolted forward at a dead gallop. The pounding hooves caused the brave to take his eye off Lydia for an instant.

That was all the opening the woman needed. She lashed out with her lariat, catching the brave across the face. Angered, the Apache turned back to her. By then it was too late for him.

Slocum had ridden close enough to launch himself through the air. The impact of his shoulder hitting the brave's rock-hard belly shook Slocum—but it knocked the Apache off his horse. Slocum tumbled after him and came up on top. Two quick punches rocked the Indian. Then a quick slash with his knife ended the brave's life amid a gurgle and gush of blood from his severed throat.

"Oh," Lydia said. She stared at the dead body, but Slocum had no time for her to feel sick.

He cleaned his knife by plunging it into the dirt beside

the corpse, then shoved it back into the sheath inside his boot. Slocum got to his feet and made a grab for the woman. His strong arm circled her waist and carried her out of the saddle. She was too startled to protest. Her horse neighed in fright and ran away, Slocum's mare close behind.

"My horse!" Lydia cried.

Slocum clamped his hand over her mouth to silence her. He pushed her back. They tumbled and fell heavily to the ground, his weight pinning her down. She struggled to get out from under him, but he held her tightly.

"Don't struggle," he whispered urgently. "For your life, stop fighting me."

Slocum had heard what Lydia hadn't. Indians came to see what the ruckus was. The two horses galloping away had distracted them. As he looked up, he saw the braves' silhouettes as they approached. Then both warriors wheeled about and chased after the horses.

"They'll take Star!"

"Your horse?"

"What else?" Lydia demanded angrily. She struggled again, but Slocum refused to let her go free. His face was only inches from hers. He hadn't noticed before how bright her reddish-brown eyes could be. They shone in the night like beacons.

"Keep your voice down," Slocum said, "and I'll let you up. Just don't move around much and draw attention to us."

"How gracious of you," she said sarcastically. When he rolled to the side, she sat up and tried to pull up her ripped, dirty dress. He couldn't help noticing a fair amount of bare breast through the disarray. "Be a gentleman and look away," she said when she noticed his interest. Lydia tried to pull up the dress to cover her nakedness and finally realized there was no way she could repair the rents. She gave up in disgust, glaring at Slocum as if challenging him to make some lewd comment.

As interested as Slocum was in her bare flesh, he was more interested in keeping them both alive. He grabbed her wrist and tugged, drawing her in the direction of the canyon wall. When Lydia tried to stand, he pulled her back low.

"Crawl," he said.

"Never!"

He stared at her for an instant, then laughed. This made her even madder when she realized what he had meant. Furious, she obeyed. On hands and knees she scampered off, finding refuge in a deep fissure at the side of the canyon.

He joined her a few minutes later after taking the time to rear up like a prairie dog and look for the Apaches. The Indians were nowhere to be seen.

"We might be in luck. They must think we've all high-tailed it up the trail, and they're satisfied with taking our horses and the cattle."

"Star," she moaned. "I won't lose my horse!"

"You'd die for that horse?"

"If I have to!"

Slocum heaved a sigh. He was a complete fool for what he was thinking. This wasn't his fight, and he didn't owe the Tewksburys anything. Not a one of them, including Lydia. But it was no surprise when he opened his mouth and heard the dreaded words pouring out.

"I'll get the horse back from them," he said. "I don't know how, but I will."

"Why?" she asked.

"I don't know," Slocum said. "I'm not responsible for the jam you got yourselves into, but I'll get the damned horse."

"Star isn't a damned horse. He's the best horse in the whole Tonto Basin!"

"Gelding?"

Lydia started to say something, clamped her mouth shut, then tittered.

"Sorry, I wasn't expecting you to ask that. Yes, Star's a gelding. Why?"

"I need to know which horse to steal back."

"Star's got a blaze on his forehead and a large black marking on his right front leg. And—"

"That's all I need to know," Slocum said, swearing that he would never do anything this stupid again and realizing he might never have the chance because he would be dead. He touched the ebony handle of his Colt, but the six-shooter was empty. Whatever he did, the knife was going to be his only weapon unless he managed to steal a rifle or pistol from a dead Apache.

He considered returning to the one whose throat he had just slit, then decided that was too dangerous. Calling attention to the body was a sure way of getting the rest of the war party down on his neck. They wouldn't even know they had lost another of their band until they gathered around their campfire to brag on how they had stolen horses and cattle from the white-eyes.

"You get up the trail to the rim and tell your pa to get on back to the Circle T. I'll find you there."

"It's not hard. We're smack in the middle of the basin. Finest grassland in the world," Lydia said proudly.

"You wait there for me. It might take a spell to steal back your horse."

Slocum stopped and looked at the woman again. In spite of dirt on her face and more than a little blood, some of it hers, she looked like an angel come to earth. He thought of kissing her but didn't.

She kissed him, then looked startled that she could have done such a thing. Without a word, Lydia covered her mouth with her hand, then bolted for the trail leading to the top of the canyon.

He watched her go, but she vanished into the darkness within seconds. Slocum thought he saw an occasional flash of white—her naked breast?—on the trail, but it might have been his imagination. He sank down with his back to the cold, rugged rock and worked through plans in his head on how best to get the horse.

He gave up making any plan until he got the lay of the land. It might be impossible. Or the war chief might be feeling cocky, so that stealing Star and his own mare would be a breeze. Slocum figured the actual rematch between him and the Indians would be something between those two extremes.

Heaving himself to his feet, Slocum set out at a quick walk, alert for the Apaches. By the time he reached the mouth of the box canyon, he knew they had retreated with their spoils. This made his mission even harder since their camp was some distance away and he was on foot, but he grimly kept slogging along, and reached the Apache bivouac just before sunrise. Tired and footsore, Slocum noted that the Indians hadn't bothered putting sentries out. He wondered what the scene had been like when the chief's son had returned empty-handed with a passel of pissed off braves riding behind him.

He forced himself to concentrate on the surroundings, on being quiet in spite of being tired to the bone, wanting to rush and get the hell away. Boldness had won the day before. Now he had to rely on stealth. Slocum worked his way around the camp where the Apaches slept fitfully. He caught his breath and held it until his heart pounded so hard he was sure it would explode when the chief's son suddenly sat up, threw off his blanket and stared straight at Slocum. Whatever had awakened the young brave had nothing to do with Slocum's lack of skill.

The youth got to his feet and paced around the camp, his face a mask of pure fury. For a moment Slocum thought he was going to witness a son killing his father. The young warrior stopped where the chief slept, drew his knife and held it high, as if he meant to plunge it downward into an unsuspecting heart. Whatever went through his head passed. The young man jammed his knife back into the sheath at his waist and stalked away.

Slocum sank behind a creosote bush and slowly let out the breath he had held. The young buck headed in the direction opposite where the horses were corralled, but Slocum knew the restlessness might bring him around and find Slocum stealing the horses. In the distance he heard cattle lowing and thought that might be the chief's son's destination. It would be daylight in another half hour. Slocum had to work fast at being a horse thief.

He shook his head. Was it being a thief to steal back your own property? Of course it wasn't, he assured himself, but he wasn't going to stop with his and the Tewksburys' mounts. He wanted all the Apaches' horses. It was only fitting payment for all he had been through.

He neared the corral made from rope strung between mesquite trees. His mare trotted to him immediately, and he gentled her.

Seeing one of the herd cozying up to the newcomer silenced the rest of the horses. Slocum spent another few minutes with his horse, saddling her and wondering what he ought to do about the Tewksburys' gear. There hardly seemed any point saddling horses that wouldn't carry riders, since it would only slow them. Getting their horses back ought to be plenty good enough.

Slocum retrieved the lariat Lydia had used to lash at her attacker, thinking it was ironic justice that the same rope would be used to drive off the remainder of the horses. Gripping the rope, he started to mount. Foot in stirrup, Slocum had started to pull upward when his sixth sense warned him of danger. That hair-bristling-on-the-back-of-his-neck feeling had kept him alive through the war, and it did so now, too.

Rather than boosting himself into the saddle, Slocum used the stirrup to fling himself parallel to the horse and behind. He hit the ground hard and spooked the mare. She kicked out at him—and this saved him. The chief's son had crept up behind him, knife in hand. If Slocum had tried to get into the saddle, he would have gotten a knife in the back halfway up.

As it was, the spooked horse reared and kicked, spun about and tossed its head, making it difficult for the brave to get at Slocum.

With a soundless cry of rage, the young warrior stepped back to let the horse get out of the way. This was all the time Slocum required to draw his Colt Navy and point it straight at the man.

They both froze, the Apache with a knife held high and Slocum with his empty six-shooter pointed at the warrior.

"No," the Indian said.

Slocum got to his feet, keeping the six-gun leveled. The brave had no way of knowing the weapon was useless. If Slocum kept the bluff running long enough, he could get away.

The Apache's rage outweighed any sense of survival. With a roar, the young man rushed Slocum. Not having time to draw his own knife, Slocum slipped to the side and let the descending knife slash past his head harmlessly. Swinging the six-shooter with all his might, Slocum landed the barrel on the Apache's wrist. The knife went spinning away, but the Indian wasn't giving up, even with a broken hand. He grappled with Slocum. The two of them crashed to the ground, with the younger man on top.

Slocum lost his grip on his Colt, but his right hand was free. He knew the fight couldn't last very long. The ruckus would awaken the rest of the war party and his eventual death would not be very pretty or quick. He took a blow to his cheek that rattled him, but his fingers closed around the hilt of the knife sheathed at his boot top.

The fight ended as abruptly as it had started. Slocum slid the blade between the brave's ribs and penetrated his heart. A convulsive shudder passed through the chief's son, then he fell to one side, dead. Panting, Slocum got to his feet, grabbed his empty six-shooter and shoved it into his holster, vowing to get ammo and reload as soon as possible. He tracked down his mare and vaulted into the saddle, then used his knife one last time to slash the ropes forming the crude corral and make certain he cut out Lydia's horse.

With a loud yell, Slocum got the horses running northward. Sooner than he would have liked, bullets sang in his direction through the burgeoning dawn. But he was away and had the Apaches' horses. They could follow, but it would be on foot. He knew Apache warriors could run all day through the desert and then fight a fierce battle, but he wanted enough distance between him and them to make it less likely.

It took Slocum four days to finally leave the angry band of Tonto Apaches behind. They had run after him on foot, as he had feared, looking to avenge the multiple disgraces he had heaped on their heads. Killing the chief's son had been bad, but worse was stealing their horses since it reflected so badly on all of them.

They were off the reservation and intent on raiding. An Apache on foot wasn't able to execute the lightning-fast strikes he was accustomed to making. Slocum guessed the cavalry was also on their trail. This made the loss of the horses even more worrisome, but worst of all was the prick to their pride. Horses were wealth, and Slocum had impoverished them.

He had ridden hard and done what he could to cover the trail left by the two dozen horses he herded ever northward. He doubted his work amounted to a hill of beans with the sharp-eyed, trail-wise Indians, but he had to try. When he reached a double-rutted road leading into the Tonto Basin, he took it gladly.

Slocum rode up the steep road until he reached a summit overlooking what might have been the most beautiful country he had ever laid eyes on. The grassland and rolling hills stretched as far as he could see, green and lush and inviting. He didn't have to urge the horses on after he saw this pastureland. They raced one another to the grass. He let them graze for an entire day before moving them on, wondering how he was going to find the Circle T Ranch. It turned out that there wasn't much to it. As he rode along the rutted road, he saw a wooden sign shot full of bullet holes. In spite of the destruction, he gleaned the directions to the Circle T.

He dropped a rope over the neck of Lydia's horse to be sure it didn't wander off now that it was getting close to home. He wanted to be the one who presented her with the prancing horse. He had to admit that the gelding was a beautiful piece of horseflesh—and he remembered the way Lydia had kissed him before rushing back to her pa and brother. While it might be out of the question for any more reward than this, he wasn't going to pass up the chance to find out exactly how grateful the auburn-haired beauty could be for the return of her prize horse.

Another hour riding brought Slocum to a gate that hung open, partly ripped from its hinges. Again the Circle T sign had been shot up, worrying Slocum a mite. Someone in the Tonto Basin had a quarrel with Tewksbury. Over the years Slocum had found that wasting ammo on a sign eventually led to bullets being exchanged with the person putting up the sign.

"Come on, you mangy cayuses," Slocum shouted, circling his small remuda and getting the stolen horses headed toward a stand of trees where he suspected the Circle T ranch house might be hidden away. He hadn't ridden a quarter mile when he heard gunfire. His hand jerked toward his Colt Navy, then slipped away. Whatever the squabble, he wasn't going to be able to help out, unless he threw his six-shooter at someone.

Slocum considered finding some safe spot and waiting for the gunfire to die down, but after the first shot, there wasn't any more.

"Might be a rancher shooting a varmint," Slocum said, but the evidence of the blown-apart signs made him doubt that. He kept a steady pace up the road that wound about and finally gave him a good view of a modest house about where he expected it at the edge of the stand of pines.

Two men stood nose to nose. One held a six-gun in his hand and the other gripped a long-barreled shotgun. Slocum recognized Tewksbury as the one holding the scattergun.

He rode closer and stopped a dozen yards away. He didn't want to intrude, but it was impossible not to spy on their hot words. Both were shouting.

"You done it, Tewksbury, I know you did, and I want 'em back. Every last one!"

"I didn't steal none of your scrawny cows, Tom. I don't have to. I got plenty of my own."

"You rustled them cattle. I know you did. Where'd you go? Where'd you get back from if you didn't take my stolen cattle to sell outside the Basin?"

"I was after strays, Tom," Tewksbury said, glaring. "Me and my kids were out."

"Caleb? Who else? Which of your other worthless spawn was with you?"

"You callin' my daughter worthless?"

"She's nuthin' but a cheap whore! Ain't she? Admit it, Tewksbury. Lydia's a nickel-a-tumble whore!"

Slocum rode forward, dismounted and went to stand beside Tewksbury. Neither of the other men noticed him until he squared off, facing the man who had just called Lydia Tewksbury a whore.

"I brought back Miss Lydia's horse," Slocum said. His cold eyes locked with Tom's startled, wide-set brown eyes.

"Who the hell are you?"

"Could ask the same," Slocum said.

"Tom Graham, that's who this is, Slocum," Tewksbury said.

"Sorry to hear about your forthcoming condition, Graham," Slocum said.

This confused Tom Graham.

"What are you saying?"

"It's mighty hard to ride with a bullet through your heart. Apologize to Mr. Tewksbury for calling Miss Lydia names, then be on your way."

"You—" Graham made the mistake of trying to lift the six-gun and shoot Slocum. A single quick step forward let Slocum grab the man's brawny wrist. Slocum twisted the gun away as it discharged. Then he punched Graham as hard as he could in the middle of his face. His nose broke and sent a shower of blood everywhere, but Slocum ig-

nored that. He had been riding with pent-up emotions after
coming on Tewksbury and his brood almost a week earlier,
and this gave him the opportunity to vent.

"You busted my nose!"

Slocum twisted a little harder and pried the pistol from
Graham's hand. He thrust the cold bore into the man's
forehead.

"I can make all the pain go away. Or you can tuck your
tail between your legs and get the hell off the Circle T. Fact
is, it doesn't matter to me which it is."

Graham grabbed for his pistol, but Slocum pulled it
back just far enough for the man to miss.

"I'll keep this as payment for all those shot-up signs
along the road."

"I didn't blow them into splinters. It was other ranchers,
other good folks who've had their beeves rustled by—"

Slocum stepped forward and Tom Graham let out a
yelp. He grabbed his horse's reins and left, shouting curses
as he went.

"Mighty friendly neighbors you got," Slocum said,
keeping his eye on Graham as the man rode away.

"Tom?" Tewksbury laughed harshly. "He's the friend-
liest of the lot. You ought to see the rest."

Slocum suspected that he just might before he left the
Tonto Basin.

4

"You didn't have to git yerself involved in this squabble, Slocum," Tewksbury said, shaking his head. He lifted his shotgun, sighted along the barrels, then lowered it. "Too far fer a good shot," he explained.

"Did you rustle his cattle?" Slocum asked. He didn't care if Tewksbury had or not. That would have been the pot calling the kettle black if he did, since he had been known to drive off a few extra head from time to time himself.

"This is 'bout the best grazin' land in the world, Slocum," Tewksbury said. "Fences get knocked down now and agin, and some of them beeves don't carry much in the way of brands."

"I understand," Slocum said, and he did. Not every rancher followed his cattle around open range close enough to brand the calves. While the law might say those calves belonged to whoever owned the cow, Slocum saw it a bit differently—and so did Tewksbury.

"Looks like you been keepin' busy since you left us," Tewksbury said. " 'Fore I go on, and I do at great lengths, I want to thank you fer knockin' some sense into that bull-headed girl of mine. Tryin' to save that horse of hers the way she did was 'bout the stupidest thing I ever heard."

"I'll go you one better. I stole the horse back from the

Apaches. Fact is, I got some Indian ponies to sell, too. You in the market for a few head of horses?"

"Indian ponies, eh?" Tewksbury said. He went to one horse and ran his hand over its back, then down its flanks. "Needs fleshin' out. Kinda skinny. Always hard to saddle-break 'em, too. Damned Indians don't use saddles too often, though this bunch must have. Or maybe they just stole these swayback nags from settlers."

Tewksbury's fingers lingered over the brand on the horse's rump. He looked at Slocum.

"Stole all of them from the Apaches," Slocum said. "Where they got 'em doesn't matter a whole lot." He shrugged. He knew they were all stolen from settlers or travelers along Arizona byways, because no reasonable Indian agent would ever allow his wards to keep their horses. Otherwise, the Apaches would be riding off on raids every morning. As it was, they seemed to slip away with distressing regularity.

"Them Apaches likely to come here huntin' fer their horses?"

Slocum didn't answer. He thought the chief could figure out where his stolen horses had been taken, but if the cavalry caught up with the war party, the chief would have bigger worries. Slocum hoped that by now the chief had his hands full with every soldier from Fort Apache, though the cavalry from that post usually dealt with keeping the Coyotero Apaches under control. It wasn't much of a stretch to think that company would be called out to go after the Tontos.

"Don't make no never mind," Tewksbury said.

"No, it doesn't."

"Ten dollars a head," Tewksbury said.

"What am I offered for that one?"

"God in Heaven, you got Star! I thought you was jist flappin' yer gums when you said you went after Lydia's horse." Tewksbury pushed his way through the herd and got to the gelding, still carrying Slocum's lariat around the neck. Tewksbury scooped up the rope and tugged.

"Will this change what you'll offer for the rest of the horses? Including yours?"

"You got my Sunfisher, too? I'll be damned, Slocum. You do! And Caleb's horse, too. You robbed them red varmints of the lot of our horses." Tewksbury turned and faced Slocum. "I'll go you one better'n buyin' the horses off you. I'll offer you a damn job, Slocum. You're better than good."

"Would that put me in the middle of a range war?" Slocum glanced over his shoulder in the direction Tom Graham had ridden. "Right about now, I'm more interested in some peace and quiet."

"Oh, don't worry yer head none 'bout Graham. He's full of hot air. He's got some nervy relatives, but they don't get too het up over what goes on out on the range."

"Why's that?" Slocum saw the answer on Tewksbury's face. Graham's relatives were inclined to ride on the wrong side of the law and didn't want to stir up too much of a dust cloud where they hid out. This made Slocum all the more eager to ride on through the Tonto Basin and head north into Utah or even Montana. It was cooler there, and he'd had his fill of desert heat and Apache bullets.

Though the Tonto Basin was mighty inviting country.

It became even more so when he saw Lydia Tewksbury come from the house. She stopped, stared and then dropped her load of laundry and ran out to fling her arms around Star's neck, kissing him. Slocum felt a twinge of jealousy.

She led the horse to within a few feet of where Slocum stood with her father. The woman stared at him, her beguiling reddish brown eyes shining with an inner glow.

"You kept your promise. I'm sorry I doubted you."

"You don't know me," Slocum said, "but my word's my bond."

"I can see that, Mr. Slocum," she said. All the while she spoke, she kept her arms around the horse's neck, as if releasing him might cause the Apaches to steal him once more.

"I jist offered Slocum here a job. He ain't said if he'd

take it yet." Tewksbury eyed him slyly. "What'll it take to make you stay? Fer a spell?"

"I was heading north," Slocum said.

"That's across country Graham owns. You might find that a bit hard to ride over since that run-in with him."

"Run-in?" demanded Lydia. "What happened? I didn't know Tom was here."

"Slocum ran him off. Good thing, too, or I'd've filled his worthless hide with buckshot. Waste of good lead."

"I can always ride west," Slocum said.

"Graham's got relatives that way."

"East?"

Tewksbury shrugged. "Don't rightly know what you'd find that direction."

"And south are the Indians," Lydia said, getting into the spirit of the dickering. "Why don't you pitch your gear in the bunkhouse, at least for a day or two? See if you like the Circle T." The look she gave him made Slocum wonder if it would be possible not to like what the Circle T had to offer. Against his better judgment he heard himself saying he would stay.

"Oh, good!" cried Lydia. He thought she was going to throw her arms around his neck and give him a kiss like she had her horse, but she refrained. Slocum wondered how itchy a trigger finger her pa had when it came to defending her virtue. The Tewksburys all had minds of their own, and a kiss might not set well with the patriarch running the ranch.

"You kin ride around fer a day or two and get the lay of the land. While you're out there—to the west—look for strays. There are a couple ponds where they gather when they wander off."

Slocum led his mare to the corral and got the rest of the Apache remuda into the corral, also. He stowed his gear in the bunkhouse, wondering where the rest of the hands were.

"Come on up to the house for dinner, won't you, Mr. Slocum?"

He looked up from tending his boots to see Lydia outlined in the doorway. For a heart-stopping moment, he thought she wasn't wearing any clothes. Then he realized her blouse was skintight and she wore a man's jeans, though better than any man Slocum had ever seen.

"That's mighty kind of you," he said. "Where're the others?" He indicated the empty bunks.

"Out on the range. Pa's always got them riding fence or looking for strays. Hardly anybody stays around the ranch house to keep me company."

Slocum heard more than the woman's words. She got a little breathless, and he saw how her chest rose and fell faster than usual. Lydia saw how he stared at her and turned sideways, outlining herself at a different angle. This way he saw tiny hard nubs pressing into the thin cotton blouse. She was getting excited.

So was Slocum.

"Might be I should do as your pa said."

"What's that?"

"Go look around a mite. Find the watering holes. Look for strays."

"You good with that rope?" She pointed to the lariat curled up and dangling from his bunk.

"Usually catch what I try to rope," he said.

"There's a lake not a mile from here where you might be able to rope something really fine in an hour or so."

"You show me?" he asked.

Lydia laughed. "Oh, yeah, Slocum, I'll show you. If you can find me, I'll show you anything you want." With that promise, the woman disappeared. It took all of Slocum's willpower not to follow her.

He slowly finished getting the scuffs out of his boots and looked at them critically. It had been a spell since he had tended them—or had a reason to. He smiled slowly. As good as it was having decently polished boots, he didn't think that was what would impress Lydia most. Slocum tended his gunbelt, then slung it around his waist, settled it and thrust in the Colt Navy. The weight reassured him.

Slocum took his sweet time fetching his mare, saddling the horse and riding out slowly to the west. A stand of juniper some distance off hinted that there might be a pool of water nearby, and he headed directly for it. When he was almost there, he saw hoofprints in the mud. Slocum knew they were fresh from the sharpness of the impression—and he suspected that Star had made the prints, since the horse hadn't been in the corral when he left.

He walked his horse into a draw and down a ravine to a grassy area running down to the edge of a lake. A tumble of rocks thrust out into the water, cutting off the view around the water. Slocum dismounted and studied the tracks. Lydia had headed for the rocks. That suited Slocum just fine. He hobbled his mare to let her graze on the grass, then started hiking into the rocks.

He emerged on the top of the hill overlooking the lake. Slocum went to the edge and peered down twenty feet into the water, hunting for Lydia. He didn't see her. He turned and stopped dead. She had come up silently behind him and stood buck naked in the warm afternoon sunlight.

"You're overdressed," she said.

"You don't waste any time, do you?" Slocum said. He felt himself growing hard just looking at her. The woman had a perfect body, marred only here and there with dark moles obvious against her white skin. She reached up and cupped her breasts, letting her fingers slowly move to her nipples. She squeezed lightly on those taut buds, duplicating the hardness Slocum had seen earlier thrusting upward against her blouse.

"There's a time to be patient and a time to take what you want. I'm tired of being patient. I want you, John." Lydia moved forward with liquid grace. He saw the play of her muscles as she came to him, the slight jiggle of her high, firm breasts, the way her auburn hair caught the sunlight and turned into red gold. But he stared at her face, those entrancing eyes and the slightly parted lips. She came into his arms and he kissed her. Or did she kiss him? Slocum couldn't figure it out. Either way, it was what they both wanted.

She pressed warmly against him, and he began to *feel* overdressed. Her lips opened and her tongue slipped out to race around his lips before plunging boldly inward to duel with his tongue. Their breathing became more strained as their pulses raced in unison. He pulled her closer. His hands stroked up and down her bare back, tracing out the bones in her spine, then moving lower to cup her firm buttocks.

He pulled her against his body even harder.

Her own hands knocked off his hat and stroked through his lank black hair before slipping around to the back of his head to hold him firmly in place as they kissed. Breaking apart after a long kiss, she pulled back enough to look up at him with half-closed eyes.

"Nice," she said. "For a start."

"You started ahead of me," Slocum said. His fingers lightly stroked over her bare ass and then around to her belly. Slipping down a few inches brought him to a tangled auburn nest already moist with her inner juices.

"You took forever getting here," she said accusingly. "What happened? You have to clean your gun?" Lydia reached down between them, unbuckled his gunbelt and let it fall to the ground. Slocum didn't notice. The woman's nimble fingers worked on the buttons holding his jeans closed. When she popped the last of the buttons on his fly, he sprang out, hard and proud and ready.

"My, my, look at this tasty morsel," she said. Sinuous as a snake, she slithered down his body to her knees, her lips brushing against the tip of his quivering manhood. She kissed lightly, then let her tongue flick out quicker than any snake's. Tremors passed through Slocum's body, and he felt weak in the legs. He reached down and ran his fingers through the lustrous strands of her hair, moving so that he could guide her in a rhythm that excited him more and more.

Her tongue and lips touched him wetly, but her teeth

lightly scoring the sides of his shaft caused the tremor to turn into an earthquake. He had to push her away. Otherwise, he would have seemed like a young buck with a woman for the first time.

"That's some mouth you have on you," he said.

"You noticed." Lydia started to dive back, but Slocum kept her away. Staring down at her caused him to tighten even more. The sunlight shone on her bare breasts and the hard red nubs capping them cast little shadows. His mouth watered at the thought of tasting them.

"My turn," he said. Slocum stripped off his shirt while Lydia worked to get his jeans down his legs. He sat heavily on the ground while she pulled at his boots and then finally got him free of his pants.

"Stay down," she said, pushing him onto his back. She bent again, her hot breath like a forest fire on his belly. She licked and kissed and worked back to the throbbing pillar between his legs. Slocum swallowed and worked to enjoy her oral touches even while fighting to hold back the fiery torrents mounting within him.

"Don't you want more than that?" he asked.

"Are you the one who can give it to me?"

He grinned from ear to ear. That was a question he could answer mighty fast. Reaching down, he took her shoulders and pushed her back onto the grass. Lydia flopped and her legs opened wantonly for him.

"Come on in," she said. "It's a nice warm, wet day."

"Yeah, it is," he said, moving into the vee of her strong legs and pressing his mouth firmly against her. She let out a tiny yelp of pleasure as his tongue invaded her inner fastness. Like a cat lapping up cream, he tended every spot thoroughly, pressing and sucking, tonguing and batting about the tiny spires of pink flesh poking up. Lydia lifted her hips and arched her back. He moved in closer, his hands gripping her buttocks and kneading them like giant lumps of firm dough. Adding the action of his mouth against her most tender flesh caused her to gasp, moan and then tense as ecstasy ran throughout her slender body.

"Oh, yes, John, that was what I needed," she said.

"That was what *you* needed," he said. "Now I'll get what I need."

"Promises, promises," she said.

"And you're going to deliver," he said.

"My word's my bond."

"No bonds this time," he said, moving up her body the way she had worked down his. He felt the tip of his engorged manhood brush where his mouth had been a moment earlier. She rocked back and lifted her knees. Then he sank easily full-length into her. For a moment, neither moved. Then they both gasped with the tightness of the fit and the heat boiling from their bodies.

He withdrew an inch, two, more, until only the thick head of his shaft remained within her. Then he smoothly stroked forward, again filling her. He relished the silken feel of her inner flesh and the moistness and the way she sobbed and moaned and begged for more.

He gave her more. Lots more. He began moving like a human piston until his arousal broke free of his control. He lost all sense of rhythm and began wildly moving, thrusting hard and giving her what she was pleading for. Slocum felt himself explode as she clamped her legs around his waist and tensed, keeping him buried deeply within her. They rolled over and over in the grass, hips moving the barest amount but giving both of them the ultimate in human pleasure.

All too soon the tension left their bodies and they lay side by side in the grass, letting the sun warm them and erase their sweat. Lydia idly dragged her fingertips over his chest, playing with the hair. Slocum began stroking over her chest.

"Yours is nicer," he said.

"No hair," Lydia said. "Not like this. I love the feel of it against my fingers and lips." She bent over and kissed him.

"But not as much as I like doing this." He caught one nipple between thumb and forefinger and rolled the fleshy nip about until it began to harden.

"More," she said hoarsely. "I want more."

"Greedy, aren't you?"

"Yes!"

Slocum got to his knees to reposition himself. He wasn't sure he could perform again so soon, but Lydia was determined. Somehow they moved closer and closer to the edge of the cliff above the lake.

"It's a long way down," he said, looking over the edge. "At least fifteen feet."

"There's something I always wanted to try," Lydia said. "Stand up."

"I am."

"On your feet," she said. She grabbed him in such a way that he had to obey. When they were standing, she pressed into him, lifted her leg and wrapped it around his waist so their crotches were intimately close.

"What now?" Slocum asked.

"Hang on. This is going to be one hell of a ride!" Lydia exclaimed. With a sudden turn that caught Slocum off-balance, they fell through the air and splashed loudly into the lake. Sputtering and thrashing about, Slocum found they were still entwined when he got to the surface.

"That wasn't anything I've ever done before," he said.

"Me, either, but I have done this."

And she showed him. Slocum wondered if there was any better place in the world than the Tonto Basin.

5

Slocum stretched out naked in the grass, letting the sun dry the water from his body. Lydia lay with her head resting on his chest. There might have been a more perfect way to spend the afternoon, but Slocum couldn't think what it was.

Yet, in spite of the lovely woman and the warm reception he had received from her father, Slocum's mind wandered as he thought of moving on. The Tonto Basin was appealing territory, but he had a wanderlust that couldn't be sated by acres of pastureland and lakes of sweet water. Even a frisky filly like Lydia wasn't likely to tie him down long. There wasn't anything ahead of him but the horizon, and that was good enough.

"What started the feud with Graham?"

"What?" Lydia stirred. She had been half-asleep. Her hand pressed down in the middle of his chest as she pushed herself upright. The sight of her nakedness caused Slocum to lose his train of thought for a moment.

"Graham didn't barge in on your pa and get so hot under the collar for the first time. Something's riled him. Your pa hinted that he might have rustled some of Graham's cattle."

"Pa's not above that," Lydia said, surprising him with her honesty. She swung her legs around, crossed them and sat facing him. "Truth is, before we came here to the Basin, we moved a lot because of the law. Badges and Tewksburys never got along too well."

"You're mighty free with that information."

Lydia shrugged. "No reason to fib about it. Nothing to be proud of, but nothing to hide, either. Since we drifted into Arizona, things have gone well for us. Ma died down in Texas before we came here. That might have been part of the problem. She was always nagging Pa about wanting more. We had a run of bad luck. Drought, disease, splenic fever in the herd—it all came crashing down on our heads."

"So you moved here," Slocum said. "You didn't bring any cattle with you?"

Lydia laughed and said, "Don't worry about the fever. We got here with little more than the clothes on our backs. That and our horses. That's one reason I'm so attached to Star. Reminds me of back home in Texas."

"So you didn't bring Texas fever with you?"

"John, really. What cattle we have were all born and bred right here in Arizona."

Or stolen here, Slocum thought, but he didn't put that into words.

"What about you? What brings you this way?"

Slocum hesitated. He didn't like talking about himself much, but Lydia had been honest with him. He should be with her, too.

"I rode with Quantrill during the war," he said, seeing the shock on her face. The Tewksburys might be from Texas and might even have supported the rebel cause, but few condoned Quantrill's viciousness. It had always amused Slocum to think that Quantrill was Ohio born and bred and had turned on other Yankees with a brutality that still festered, even this long after the war.

"You liked riding with him?"

Slocum touched a pair of round scars on his belly, hardly knowing he did so.

"I complained about what he did in Lawrence, and he had Bill Anderson gut-shoot me. It took months to recover.

When I did, I went home to Georgia and found a carpet-bagger judge had taken a fancy to the family farm."

"That's why you drifted west?" Lydia knew him well enough to know he wasn't the kind to abide by such thievery. He had shot and killed the judge and his hired gunman and ridden out, a federal warrant on his head. A man could do a powerful lot of evil things, but somehow killing a crooked judge who needed it was worse than most in the eyes of the law.

"Been laying back in meadows with beautiful, naked woman and watching the clouds fly by ever since."

Her fingers traced the lines of his jaw, down lower and across his shoulders and biceps.

"A real lackadaisical life," she said. "Doing nothing's made you strong and hard. From the worn look of that six-gun of yours, it does about the same nothing."

Slocum began to feel a little uneasy. Lydia saw him a little too clearly. He was no gunfighter, but he was faster than most and wasn't reluctant about using the Colt Navy. During the war he had been a sniper and hadn't balked any at squinting down a barrel, waiting most of a day and then taking one shot that killed a Yankee officer before he even knew there was a Johnny Reb within a mile.

"I told your pa I'd ride around and hunt for strays. He said to check the fence, too."

Lydia laughed and shook her head. Auburn hair floated in the light breeze and formed a mahogany mist around her head, lit by the sun and making her about the loveliest thing Slocum could remember seeing.

"Don't strain too much hunting for fences. The other ranchers put them up. Pa and Caleb never quite get around to it. The rest of the cowboys don't cotton much to hard work like that, either."

"The Circle T sounds like a good place not to work," Slocum said. "Is the pay any good?"

"About the same as the work. Nobody gets rich working for the Tewksburys, but nobody has much to complain about, otherwise."

Slocum understood. John Tewksbury wasn't—quite—a rustler, but most of his beeves had probably carried another ranch's brand at one time.

"If this afternoon is any indication of the pay, I'd say it's about as fine as anything in all Arizona Territory," Slocum said. He sat up and kissed Lydia's breast. Or tried to. She leaned back so he missed by inches.

"None of that," she said.

"That wasn't what you said a while ago," Slocum pointed out.

"You got work to do, and Pa will be all antsy if I don't show up soon." There was a serious note to Lydia's words that made Slocum think there was something darker going on in the Basin. Before he could ask, she lithely swung around, got to her feet and vanished behind some bushes. In a few minutes, she emerged, working to get her clothing into order.

"You ride around naked?" she asked. Lydia kicked his shirt and pants toward him. "See you back at the house. Dinner's served around six. You got a watch?"

Slocum fumbled in his vest pocket and showed her his watch. It had been his brother Robert's and was his only legacy. Robert had died during Pickett's Charge. The watch was a constant reminder of what had been lost to stupidity.

"Six," Lydia said. She blew him a kiss as she hurried down the slope. He had never seen where she had tied her horse. Within a minute, receding hoofbeats told him she had returned to the ranch.

He finished dressing, made sure his six-gun rested easy in its cross-draw holster, then followed the slope down to where he had left his horse. The mare was content, having grazed most of the afternoon.

"We're both about as happy as we can be, aren't we?" Slocum patted the mare's neck, mounted and headed southwest, riding slowly, taking in the hills and treed ravines, and mentally staking out paths to watering holes. The rest of Arizona might be dry as a bone, but the Tonto

Basin had water aplenty for both man and beast. As he rode past one deep, clear pond, he saw several deer and a cougar. Hunting would be good here. He took in the beauty and bounty of the land and found himself mentally wrestling with his urge to move on. What gear he had left in the bunkhouse wouldn't be missed, but the Circle T had everything a man could want. Why leave?

Slocum hadn't quite come up with an answer to that when he spotted three riders on a ridge ahead. He slowed his mare and watched as the trio made their way over the ridgeline and vanished from sight. He wiped his forehead and considered the three riders. He had yet to meet any of the cowboys working for Tewksbury. This might be a good time to see what they thought of riding for the Circle T. Slocum turned his horse's face and headed up the steep slope.

When he got to the ridge, he saw where the riders had gone. The three were down in a hollow working a few head of cattle. Something about the way they whooped and hollered as they circled the cattle put Slocum on guard. He had seen men who enjoyed their work, but not as much as these three. Rounding up strays ought to be dull work and not an occasion to act as these men were.

Slocum had started down the slope toward the cattle when one of the cowboys spotted him. The three rode together and exchanged hasty words. This struck Slocum as out of the ordinary. Without being too obvious, he reached across and pulled away the leather thong over the hammer of his six-shooter. If the need arose, he could let lead fly in a hurry.

"Howdy!" Slocum called.

"Who're you?" The leader of the three was unshaven and a little haggard, as if he had been on the trail for a month. His condition didn't bother Slocum as much as the way the man leaned forward and slid his rifle partly from the saddle sheath.

"Not very friendly, are you? I'm just passing through," Slocum said, not wanting to mention Tewksbury by name yet.

"Keep on ridin', stranger," the man said. He made no move to return his rifle to its scabbard. If anything, he pulled it a little farther out. Slocum saw the other two men moving their gun hands into position to throw down on him.

"Been a while since I had a decent job. What's the brand on those cows? Circle T?"

"That's the brand," the man said.

"Don't fool around with him none, Murphy," whined the man on his right. "We got work to do."

"Work's what I'm looking for. You the Circle T fore-man?" From the man's reaction, Slocum knew these three weren't Tewksbury's hands.

Rustlers. The entire Tonto Basin had to be filled with nothing but rustlers.

"What if I am?"

"Well, Mr. Murphy, I'd like to join up. Three squares a day and a place to rest my head at night sounds like heaven to me right now." Slocum hoped he wasn't too obviously lying. The three exchanged looks. Murphy squinted at him, looking more like a hunting wolf than a man now.

"You work cows before?"

"Now and then," Slocum said.

"Why don't you drive these beeves and show us what you've got?"

"Which way's the ranch house?"

"Why do you want to take 'em there?" One of Murphy's henchmen looked agitated at the notion of taking the cows to Tewksbury's house.

"Reckon you were out here," Slocum said. "There's plenty of pastureland and water. You must want them to ei-ther slaughter for food or to dip against disease. Any Texas fever from ticks in this part of the country?"

"Texas fever?" Murphy looked confused. Slocum knew then that the man wasn't a drover. Truth was, he wasn't much of a rustler, either.

Something in Slocum's expression warned the men. The two with Murphy went for their six-shooters and Murphy yanked at his rifle, pulling it free and swinging the muzzle around in Slocum's direction.

They were all a heartbeat too late. Slocum was quick, and being up against three desperadoes lent even more speed to his hand. He cleared leather and fired point-blank at the nearest rustler. The man grunted and clutched his chest. His six-gun slid from his numbed fingers and landed on a rock, discharging. This spooked his horse and caused a greater commotion than anything Slocum could have done.

"Kill 'im, shoot 'im!" cried Murphy. He fired his rifle and the slug went wild. Slocum took a more careful aim and fired, but Murphy's bucking horse ruined the shot. Slocum's bullet took off Murphy's hat but did nothing to stop him from firing his rifle again.

That shot came closer, but Slocum was bent low over his mare's neck now. He fired twice more at Murphy, then had to turn his attention to the other rustler.

They exchanged shots. Slocum felt his hat jerk and knew the brim had another hole in it. He emptied his Colt and missed with every shot. Slamming his six-shooter into its holster, he worked to unlimber the rifle he had gotten from Tewksbury to replace his own lost Winchester. The cattle stampeded, the horses reared, and hot lead flew all around, adding to the confusion.

By the time Slocum got control of his horse again, the three rustlers had hightailed it. He started after them, then paused. He took the time to fumble in his saddlebags and pull out a loaded cylinder for his pistol. Swapping the emptied one for a full load made him feel better. Slocum pulled up his rifle and sighted in time to see the three clumsy cattle thieves reach the top of the rise.

Murphy silhouetted himself against the sky. Slocum was a good shot, and the range wasn't more than a hundred yards. He aimed, squeezed the trigger and felt the recoil press into his shoulder. Even as he loosed the shot, he knew it was a good one.

Slocum lifted his head and saw Murphy throw up his hands and fall from horseback. It was a tribute to cowardice that the two men with him both galloped off.

Slocum levered a new round into the rifle chamber and rode up the hill slowly. Something didn't feel right to him. He heard Murphy moaning in pain. Slocum had known his shot wasn't a killing one, but he had no idea how seriously wounded Murphy might be. The man had fallen from his horse, but might be playing possum now. If Slocum rode up bold as brass thinking he was going to finish off the rustler, he might be the one getting shot.

Rather than continue up to the ridge, Slocum rode parallel, going a couple dozen yards before cutting back for the high ground. He was glad he did. Just on the other side of the ridgeline crouched the unwounded rustler, his rifle out and aimed where Slocum would have appeared if he hadn't gotten suspicious.

"Looking for me?" Slocum asked.

The rustler jerked around, startled. Before he could train his rifle on Slocum, he caught a bullet in the gut. The rustler staggered and fell to his knees, but he was tougher than he looked. He fought to bring up the rifle and shoot Slocum. Slocum waited a moment and finally saw that the man was going to succeed through either sheer determination or outright meanness. It didn't matter which. Slocum took an easy shot. The rustler sighed and collapsed, dead.

Of the other cattle thief, Slocum saw nothing. He jumped to the ground and went to the man he had just killed. A few dollars in the rustler's vest pocket disappeared into Slocum's pocket. There was nothing else giving a hint who the man might be.

On foot Slocum went to where he had left Murphy. A small curl came to Slocum's lips. He had been right about Murphy, too. Not only had his partner waited in ambush, but Murphy wasn't all that badly hurt. Slocum's bullet had hit him in the left arm. Clutched in the man's right hand was a big six-gun.

"You lose again, Murphy," Slocum said.

The man jerked around.

"Wait, don't shoot me. I ain't worth it." He tossed away his six-shooter. "Let me go. I'll disappear and you won't never see me again."

"If I shot you where you are, I'd never see you again," Slocum said.

"Ain't worth it, mister. It ain't. You don't want to make Tom Graham mad at you. You work for Tewksbury? Graham'll offer you more money. Hell, Tewksbury ain't got two nickels to rub together."

"You work for Graham?"

"I'm his foreman."

Slocum laughed. Murphy hardly knew which end of the cow the moo came from. Calling himself a foreman insulted every other foreman on every other ranch in the West.

"You able to walk?"

"No, mister, I can't. I think I busted a leg when you shot me off my horse."

"Too bad." Slocum leveled his rifle and waited a second for the predictable answer.

"Not so fast, please," begged Murphy. "I can walk. A little. More of a hobble, but I can at least stand." He got to his feet. Slocum didn't see anything wrong with the man other than the bullet hole in his left arm.

Murphy watched nervously as Slocum considered what to do.

"Look, mister, Graham will pay you a ransom for me. I'm valuable to him."

Slocum laughed again. "You aren't even decent buzzard bait. If they dined on you, they'd puke out their guts. I have too much respect for buzzards to let them do that. Start walking. Toward Tewksbury's house."

"He'll kill me! I was rustling his cows."

"Fancy that," Slocum said. "Start hoofing it or I'll shoot you where you stand."

"You killed Barney?"

"Didn't ask his name before I shot him," Slocum said.

"Or do you mean the other yahoo? The one I gut-shot back at the herd?"

"Hate to have to tell Barney's family you killed him."

"If you don't start walking, you won't have to tell anyone anything."

Slocum waited for Murphy to begin the trek back to the Tewksbury house. He went and fetched his mare, then caught up in a few minutes. Murphy wasn't much of a rustler. He wasn't much for walking, either.

Slocum herded Graham's foreman all the way back, to let Tewksbury handle the matter.

6

"Think this is a smart thing to do?" Slocum asked. He watched a naked Murphy hopping down the road away from Circle T land. "He's going to be looking to shoot you in the back, first chance he gets."

Tewksbury laughed.

"Given the chance, that son of a bitch'd done that no matter what. Murphy is a low-down, no account, mouth-breathin' son of a bitch. Wait," Tewksbury said, scratching his chin, "I said that already. Goes to show he ain't worth the effort to think up new ways of describin' him, his habits and his mama."

"You should burn his clothes," Slocum said, looking at the pile at his feet. He didn't cotton much to humiliating a man. Better to have put a slug through Murphy's head than to do this to him, but Tewksbury knew what to do. He lived here and Slocum could always ride out.

"Where'd the lice live then?" Tewksbury asked, smiling broadly. "You got to loosen up, Slocum. Things are different here than other places."

"I noticed," Slocum said, his eyes drifting to where Lydia hung her laundry on a long line. She caught his eye and saw that her father had his back to her. She gave a wiggle, then turned and hiked up her skirts, showing

Slocum her bare bottom. Lydia dropped her skirts and went back to clothes-pinning laundry until she was sure her pa wasn't looking. Then she lifted her skirts while facing Slocum to give him a flash of auburn fur nestled between her creamy white thighs. Then she dropped her skirts, hiked up her undergarment and went back to work, as if nothing had happened.

Slocum felt stirrings that he tried to deny. He shook his head. Tewksbury was right. Things were entirely different here than elsewhere.

"Where'd you come across those varmints tryin' to rustle my cattle?"

"I was taking your advice and getting the lay of the land," Slocum said, thinking how precisely accurate that was, "and I ran into them a mile beyond the lake."

"In a draw? I think I know the place. Cattle end up there and can't seem to get out. Or maybe they's lazy animals and not wantin' to hike all the way back up that hill to get out."

"There was plenty of grazing for them. I didn't have a chance to see if there was water."

"There is, 'bout a mile deeper into that valley. Saddle up and let's go see. I kin use them beeves, especially after the redskins stole those other strays I'd rounded up."

"That's a shame," Slocum said. "Where are the rest of your cowboys? I thought Murphy and his cronies worked for you. Good thing I didn't come right out and ask or they'd have filled me with holes instead of it being the other way around."

"I ain't got a powerful lot of 'em. Caleb's gone to fetch the ones left. You're a smart galoot, Slocum, as if it took a genius to figger out the Circle T is about bankrupt. In spite of the grass, there's no market for cattle anywhere around here. Not in Prescott, not south in Tombstone, nowhere. If this was Texas, I'd know what to do. The trail drives are dyin' out there, but the railroads are there to take cattle to markets on the other side of the Mississippi. Ain't nuthin' like that 'round here."

Slocum stayed silent as they rode back to where the cattle had been bunched together for rustling. It came as a surprise when he didn't find the small herd.

"They were here. Murphy and—"

"Don't get so worked up, Slocum," Tewksbury said. "Cows got a way of vanishin' real fast around these parts."

Slocum ignored the rancher and rode to the spot where he had shot Murphy's henchman. The ground was cut up from both horse and cattle hooves. He mentally followed one set of tracks going to the ridge. Murphy and his partners were responsible for those. But other tracks came in and mingled with those from the cattle.

"That way," Slocum said, pointing down the valley. "At least two horsemen drove the cattle that way."

"Probably more of Graham's thievin' crew," Tewksbury said. "You up for a fight?"

"You don't want to get your cattle back?"

"Easier to steal some others," Tewksbury said. When he saw Slocum's shocked expression, he added, "That's the way things're done round here. Ain't sayin' it's right, but it's the way they are."

"Don't you want to know for certain who stole your cattle?"

"Don't matter that much to me, but if it does to you, let's ride. For a while." Tewksbury snapped his reins and got his swayback horse trotting in the direction Slocum had decided was going to show them the rustlers the quickest.

In less than an hour they had overtaken the thieves. Five men circled the small herd and kept them moving off the Circle T land.

"Ain't worth it, Slocum," Tewksbury said anxiously. "Five of them and only two of us."

Slocum had to agree. The men weren't as scruffy as Murphy and his men. They rode with more authority, and even at this distance Slocum could tell they kept their six-shooters ready for action. Riding up on these men, pretending to be a stranger and asking after employment would get him a bullet in the back.

"You know them?"

"Think so. Tough hombres. They don't have land around here, either, if you're thinkin' on stealin' back the beeves. Pure rustlers, mean through and through."

Slocum considered a different story to get closer to them, but he had rustled enough cattle to know what these men would do if he rode up to them. As that thought crossed his mind, he forgot about approaching them. He knew rustlers, and there wasn't any reason for them to leave witnesses. They might be related, as many of the gangs of rustlers were, and wouldn't be looking to increase their number.

"You can always tell the sheriff," Slocum said. "There is a sheriff somewhere, isn't there?"

"Over in Prescott. Not even sure what his name is, and nope, I ain't gonna ride all that way just to tell him five varmints stole a few head of my cattle. He'd laugh in my face."

"If you don't know him—"

"I don't know who wears the damn badge," he said, "but that don't mean he won't know me."

Slocum nodded slowly as he thought on that. Wanted posters had a way of staying tacked to a lawman's office wall for a powerful long time. He had been in some marshals' offices where not one of dozens of yellowed, old posters showed a living, breathing outlaw.

"What are you going to do?"

"Got me a new scheme for makin' a few dollars," Tewksbury said, "and it's honest. Don't worry none on that score, Slocum. Folks in these parts might not like it much, but my back's against the wall. If I don't do something quick to make money, I'll have to abandon the Circle T. I've done worse things in my life, but not since we come to Arizona."

"What's this moneymaking scheme?"

"Sheep," Tewksbury said. "I know, I know, I hate

them damn woollies as much as the next drover, but there's a big market for what they got. I kin even sell the wool to the Navajos and Hopis up north, as well as mutton over in Prescott. Too many cattle but not so many sheep."

"They pull up the grass by the roots. You'll turn this entire basin into a desert, like down south," Slocum said.

"That's what I hear, but a desert eventually or me and mine starvin' now?"

Slocum had no love for the smelly, bleating critters.

"I'll be riding on, if you're turning this into a sheep ranch."

"There's one other chance to keep going. You ever broke mustangs?"

"Enough," Slocum allowed.

"There's herds of wild horses runnin' throughout the Tonto Basin. If we kin catch enough, break 'em and sell 'em, well, there's more market for horses than sheep."

"Breaking horses is hard work," Slocum said. His backside hurt from the long hours he had spent in the saddle getting this far north from down in the Sonora Desert. Every bone in his body would hurt by the time he finished breaking a few horses.

"I know that," Tewksbury said, patting his horse's neck. "Ole Sunfisher here earned his name. I was the only one what could ride him. He'd buck, get all four legs off the ground and then arch his damn back, spin around in midair and then hit so hard it'd chip my teeth. Took the better part of a week to break him."

"Looks like you did a good job," Slocum said.

"This ole body ain't up fer it no more, Slocum. Caleb could do it, but his arms ain't all healed up yet. He has a way with horses, but his grip's still a mite weak to hang on tight enough to keep from gettin' bucked off more'n he's in the saddle."

"What other hands do you have?"

"Four, last I counted at dinner. But then, they might have drifted on. Never can tell who'll show up for chuck."

Slocum glanced over his shoulder in the direction of the rustlers and their small, stolen herd of Tewksbury's cattle. It galled him to let anyone ride off like that, considering those beeves belonged to the Circle T, unlike others that must be on the range.

"Where're the mustangs?"

"To the north," Tewksbury said. "You thinkin' on bustin' a bronc or two fer me?"

"How'll you pay me?"

"That is the crux of the matter, ain't it?" Tewksbury rode in silence for almost a mile before speaking again. "Beeves. You kin take whatever cows you want. If I'm gettin' out of the cattle growin' business and puttin' them smelly white puffballs in their stead, you might as well be the one who takes 'em."

"What would a cow go for over in Prescott?"

"You might git five dollars fer it. Me, I'd lose money on the deal."

"If you get twenty dollars of work out of me, you'd come out ahead."

"Somethin' like that," Tewksbury said.

"We have time. Let's scout some of those wild horses," Slocum said.

"That's talkin'! I figgered I could count on you, Slocum."

They left the trail meandering back to the ranch house and struck out north. Tewksbury chattered away like an old woman at a quilting bee, but Slocum only grunted in response now and then. He worried about what he was getting himself into. Rustlers. Sheep. A rancher who was open about being a crook.

Lydia.

No matter how many different things he considered that told him to keep riding, he kept coming back to her. She had seemed such a chaste, demure young thing. How wrong he had been. Sampling what she so willingly offered—for a week or two—couldn't be wrong, he finally decided.

"There!" cried Tewksbury. "See 'em?"

"The cloud of dust?" Slocum pulled his hat brim down to shade his eyes and noted the new bullet damage there. He ignored the hole and slowly studied the dust. It grew larger as it came toward them. Slocum pushed his hat back as the herd thundered along.

"The Tonto Basin has about anything a man could want," he said slowly. A quick count showed better than twenty head of wild horses.

"Lookee there. One of them's trailin' behind. What do you think, Slocum?"

Slocum wasn't listening. He had seen the horse, too, and was already racing forward to cut it off from the remainder of the herd. As he rode, he unfastened his lariat. The horse he had singled out trotted along, then slowed and stopped to toss its head. Slocum couldn't have asked for a better opportunity.

He rode down on the horse, his lariat spinning over his head. Judging distances and the way the horse was likely to bolt, Slocum adjusted his approach just enough. When the mustang finally started to run, it was too late. The rope spun through the air and dropped neatly over the animal's head. Slocum's mare responded perfectly. He took two quick turns around the saddle horn as the mare dug in her heels. The mustang reared. This settled the rope even more securely around its neck.

Before he could call out to Tewksbury, the man added a second rope so the mustang was effectively trapped between them.

"We make quite a team," Slocum said to Tewksbury. "This one's wild enough and strong enough that one rope wouldn't do much good." He reeled in the slack and gave the horse a chance to settle down. Slocum worried that, like the cattle, these horses might be branded, but the hip on this paint was unbranded.

"This is the easy part. Hell, me and the boys've caught more'n one of these wild beasts. Breakin' 'em is another kettle of fish."

Slocum looked over the paint's sleek lines.

"Breaking this filly's going to be fun," he said.

Tewksbury only smiled as they started back to the Circle T corral with the paint captured between them.

7

"Where's your pa?" Slocum pushed back from the breakfast table, belly full and feeling like he could whip his weight in wildcats. When Lydia didn't answer right away, he pushed away the empty tin plate and leaned forward with his elbows on the table and waited. She finally looked up from her busy work. Her ginger eyes locked with his.

"Rather not say. Pa goes off from time to time."

"Considering how touchy everyone in the territory is, he ought to take Caleb or a couple of his hands with him."

Lydia laughed harshly.

"You've seen the kind of men we have working here, John. He's better off riding alone."

"You include me in that?"

"What? Oh, no, of course not. You're quite the cowboy. You've broke five horses. Selling them will keep the Circle T in business for a while longer." Lydia wiped her hands on her apron and came around the table. She pushed the plate back even farther and perched on the edge. Slocum felt his heart pounding faster at her nearness.

Lydia lifted one leg high and swept it over his head so she straddled him, her behind resting on the table. With a little twitch, she lifted her skirt a mite.

"Go on, John," she said in a husky whisper. "See what I've got up there. Just for you."

Slocum's hand slipped under the cloth and found warm, firm leg. Slowly working his stroking fingers up to her thigh made the woman sigh. Lydia shuddered lightly and closed her eyes as she leaned back, bracing herself with both hands on the table. Her legs drifted apart even more as Slocum probed up even farther and found the tangled mat nestled between her legs. The dampness there told him she was ready for him.

She jerked upright and pushed him back so hard his chair skidded.

"Pa," she said. Her face was flushed and her gaze hot. She silently mouthed, "Later," as John Tewksbury came in.

"Mornin' all," he said, flopping into a chair. "What's fer breakfast? I'm hungry 'nuff to eat a horse."

"Luckily, we sold them, Pa," Lydia said. She stayed turned away long enough for the flush in her cheeks to fade. She dropped a plate in front of him. "Beefsteak. Same as always."

"How many of them mooin' bastards we got left to eat? I'm sick of 'em."

"Don't get too sick. I reckon you owe me twenty by now." Slocum had spoken several times with Caleb and the other hands, who assured him that he could sell a decently fattened cow for as much as eight dollars in Prescott. When he broke enough horses to get up to twenty-five cows owed him, Slocum intended to drive the small herd to Prescott, sell them and then leave.

Standing behind her father, Lydia caught Slocum's eye. She pressed her hands hard onto her breasts and then massaged enough to cause the nipples to pop up. What she did with her tongue was enough to make Slocum hard.

"More, Pa?" Lydia reached over to the counter and grabbed a plate of biscuits. She dropped those on the table in front of her father. If Tewksbury knew what his daughter did behind his back, he showed no sign as he plowed into the steak and wolfed down a hot biscuit smeared with fresh churned butter before answering.

"A shot of bourbon would go mighty good, but I reckon we ain't got none, do we?"

"Too expensive, Pa, except for use as medicine." Lydia came around and sat on the chair opposite her father. "Don't tell me you drank our medicinal supply?"

"Now, daughter, I was feelin' a whole lot of pain the other night. Put it on your list when we get supplies."

Tewksbury forked in a large hunk of meat, then turned to Slocum and said, "You up to ridin' with me? I got to talk to the Daggs boys."

"Those sheepherders?" Lydia scoffed. "They're crooks, Papa. Don't forget to count your fingers if you shake hands with either of them. I wouldn't put it past them to steal your pinky and maybe your thumb, to boot."

"They're not so bad. They know how to raise sheep and said they'd show me how to tend a herd of them cheap."

"Flock," Slocum corrected. "Cattle are in herds; sheep are in flocks. You need a sheepdog, too."

"Never liked dogs. All the time yappin' and snuffin' around. No tellin' what varmint they'd kill and bring back, either. I'll let Caleb chase them woollies around. Since he got his arms all shot up, seems the courage drained outta him." Tewksbury finished his breakfast and leaned back, satisfied. He hooked his thumbs under his suspenders, lifted them away from his ample belly and belched. "Mighty good tucker, daughter. You'll make a man a fine wife one day, the way you cook."

"Who'd marry me without a dowry, Papa?" she said with mock sweetness.

"That's what I love 'bout her. She's jist like her ma. Got quite a mouth."

"That she does," Slocum said.

"What?" Tewksbury looked at him sharply.

"I don't often hear a girl mouthing off to her pa the way Lydia does to you."

"Yeah, right," Tewksbury said. "Let's get out to meet

with them Daggs brothers. The sooner we talk to them, the sooner I can be raisin' mutton."

"Where are we supposed to meet them?" Slocum asked.

"They got a big spread up to the northeast in Flagstaff, way past Graham's spread on Cherry Creek. So we sneak through Graham land and find where them sheepherders are camped."

"That's guaranteed to make for trouble, if Graham and his men spot us," Slocum said.

"You ain't afeared of 'em, Slocum. I saw the way you faced down Tom Graham before. With an empty gun, yet!"

Slocum hadn't told the man that. He wondered if Tewksbury was good at guessing or just figured it was true after their run-in with the Apaches in the Sierra Anchas. Playing poker with Tewksbury might end up with all the chips on the other side of the table.

"We can go west to the lake and then due north. That ought to keep the peace awhile longer," said Slocum.

They rode for most of the day, Slocum warily looking for any hint that Graham saw them riding across his land. A little after sundown Slocum sniffed hard at the cool air and caught a hint of smoke.

"That's got to be them," Tewksbury said. "Take a really good whiff. They're cookin' mutton."

Slocum thought Tewksbury had to be right. They rode another half mile and found two men huddled around a campfire, poking at stew in a pot. Both reached for rifles until Tewksbury hailed them.

"No need to ventilate us, least not till we et some of that fine lamb stew."

"You must be John Tewksbury. This one of your boys?" The shorter of the two men—and neither was hardly more than five-five—pointed at Slocum.

"I'll vouch fer him. Best damned bronc buster I ever did see, and I seen some dandies," Tewksbury said. He went on garrulously while Slocum tethered their horses and sat on a log, studying the men closely.

Neither of the Daggs brothers had introduced himself, and Slocum might not have been able to keep them straight if they had. He doubted they were twins, but he wouldn't have been surprised if they declared themselves to be. Short, stocky, they moved with a slowness that reflected their lives as sheepherders. A cattleman had to be quick. A toss of a bull's head could ram a horn into a gut. Being butted by a sheep didn't carry the same penalty. And Slocum had never heard of a sheep stampede. The woollies would run a few yards, then forget what was bothering them and return to cropping the grass so close it would take a couple years to grow back—when the sheep didn't pull it out of the ground by its roots, killing it.

"You know anything about sheep?"

It took Slocum a few seconds to realize one of the Daggs had spoken to him.

"Prefer cattle," Slocum said.

"We did, too, until the Hash Knife outfit lit into us. They killed our stock, forcing us to raise sheep."

"Bet a bunch of drovers loved that," Slocum said.

"First off, they ran four thousand of our sheep into a river. Then they tied some of our sheepherders to a tree and left 'em to die. We got lucky and found them before they cooked to death in the sun. Since then, it's been a constant war."

"That's why they're wantin' me to take a few thousand sheep here," Tewksbury said. "I graze them in the Basin, they give me a cut of the profit. Not much trouble here findin' grasslands."

"What'll Graham think?"

"Who cares?" Tewksbury said. Slocum thought the rancher sounded a little too gloating. The fight between Tewksbury and Graham had a definite personal undercurrent that went beyond business.

"The market's good for sheep," one of the Daggs brothers said. "Real good. We're looking to double or triple our herd moving some sheep down into the Tonto Basin."

"I don't know anything about sheep. Neither does he," Slocum said, looking squarely at John Tewksbury. "We'll need some help, or your investment will end up as fertilizer."

"We have an expert shepherd. He's a Basque," said the other Daggs brother. "That's in Spain."

"I know that," Tewksbury said, although Slocum doubted that he did. The limits of Tewksbury's expertise were cloudy. Slocum knew he was probably a good rustler but not as good keeping herds of cattle and making a profit from them. Being in the middle of the Basin and unable to raise cattle told that much. Slocum had no idea if Tewksbury was right about market prices. He could have been, but this was nothing other ranchers hadn't faced and survived. Usually drought or disease wiped them out, not conditions that were too favorable.

"Does he speak Spanish?" Slocum asked.

The Daggs brothers glanced at each other and smiled.

"Don't go joshin' them none, Slocum," Tewksbury said. "If their boy's from Spain, of course he speaks Spanish."

"No," said the Daggs on the right. "He does speak English. A little."

Tewksbury frowned as he looked at Slocum. Whatever poker face he might have normally vanished. Slocum saw that the rancher thought Slocum and the Daggs brothers were pulling his leg.

"The Basque speak a very strange language," one brother said. "Not like Spanish. Not like anything else you ever heard. The Devil's Tongue, the Spanish call it. They do not like the Basque."

The other brother piped up. "And the Basque do not like them so much, either."

"That don't make no never mind," Tewksbury said. "We need to find out how much land the sheep'll need to graze on. What other things do we have to be on the lookout for to keep them happy?"

"They will be happiest if they are not shot and killed."

Tewksbury looked at Slocum and said, "Reckon that's

true of most livin' critters. How many do you want to move onto my land?"

"Ten thousand, to start," said one Daggs brother. "We can get them moving from Flagstaff and down here on your range by the end of the week. You'll be drawing maintenance money for them before you know it."

"I'll sell off what remains of my cattle."

Slocum wondered how many cows were left—he had worried about getting twenty as payment for his work breaking mustangs. If Tewksbury wanted to get rid of a herd, Slocum considered driving them to Prescott to get what he could for them. For a cut of the sale price.

"Shake on it," Tewksbury said, thrusting out his grimy hand. Both Daggs brothers also shook.

"I'm itchin' to git on back to the Circle T, Slocum," Tewksbury said. "Let's hit the trail."

Slocum silently followed the rancher. It was well past sundown now and the Daggs brothers had offered some of their stew. He didn't know what the rancher's hurry was leaving. He found out when they were out of earshot.

"Cain't abide by the smell of that cookin' meat. Might have to cram straw up my nose if them woollies smell as bad."

"You heard what they said about the Hash Knife outfit killing their sheep. Do you think Graham will be any more accommodating?"

"Hell, no. If anything, he'll take this as a personal insult. That means we gotta watch all the closer."

"If you want the cattle off your rangeland, I'll drive the herd to market for you. I'll take my share for breaking the horses and split the rest."

"Jist you drivin' a whole herd? You'd need a couple of my hands. Caleb, maybe, and one or two of the others."

"They'd be a big help," Slocum said.

"Not gonna happen, Slocum. Cain't spare them now that I got ten thousand sheep on the way from Flagstaff."

"Why are you in such a hurry to get back to the Circle T?"

"It shows, eh? Well, let me tell you, Slocum, there's trouble brewin', and I don't want to be too far off fer too long."

"Graham?"

"Who else? That skunk'd stink up the whole damn Basin, given the chance. And he thinks now's his time to try."

"What have you heard?"

"Herd," Tewksbury mused. "That's the word. I got Caleb and the boys out guardin' what's left of our herd, but I want to be on hand myself. You kin join in since I know you don't fancy Tom Graham much, either."

"I don't have a quarrel with him," Slocum said. He thought on it. Murphy presented a bigger problem than his boss, but Slocum realized he had chosen sides and it wasn't with Tom Graham.

"Got the bulk of the herd up near that lake where you and Graham's boys mixed it up."

They left the road and cut across the countryside. Slocum was sure they trespassed on Graham's ranch, but he said nothing. Tewksbury kept up a steady stream of meaningless chatter that eventually put Slocum on edge.

"I don't know why Graham is still a problem," Slocum said. "By now you could have talked him to death."

"Never got that close to the varmint, Slocum," Tewksbury said, laughing. "You got a good sense of humor. That's one thing I like 'bout you." Tewksbury pulled back on his reins and pointed. "Up over that there hill's the lake where the herd ought to be. You ready fer some gunplay?"

"I avoid it when I can," Slocum said, "but if Graham or anyone else tries to steal the cattle, I won't shy away from it."

"Course not. Them's your cattle. Many of 'em, at any rate," Tewksbury said, grinning crookedly. He snapped his reins and shot off, letting Slocum trail behind.

Slocum had the feeling he was riding into a tornado, but

when they reached a ridge looking down into the hollow, all seemed peaceful. Now and then a cow lowed. The bright starlight turned the valley into a gently illuminated stretch that seemed peaceful—until Slocum spotted a few cattle edging away from a wooded area.

"Something's going on over there."

"Rustlers?"

Slocum shook his head. There was no way of telling at this distance. He pulled the Winchester from its sheath and levered in a round.

"Back me up," he told Tewksbury.

"You—"

Slocum wasn't inclined to listen to the long-winded rancher. Better to tackle a dozen rustlers than hear one more story of life in Texas and how Graham was a snake in the grass. Slocum rode so he kept the bulk of the herd between him and the copse that the cattle shied from.

He reached the far side of the herd and waited. Every sense straining, Slocum tried to catch the hint of odor on the soft wind fitfully meandering across the valley. Leather. Gun oil. Horses. He didn't catch any of those scents, but the cows caught something.

Slocum rode closer and in a smooth motion brought up the rifle and fired. He missed the wolf stalking a calf at the periphery of the herd, but he ruined its chance of getting a quick meal. The cattle began to run. Slocum squeezed off a second shot but missed the wolf again. He considered going after it because it must be sick. Otherwise, it would never have stalked its prey from upwind.

"Let it go, Slocum," Tewksbury said. "There's no point goin' after it."

"What if I want a wolf skin?"

"It'll disappear like a ghost within twenty yards. I been after that gray devil for months."

Slocum doubted Tewksbury's hunting skill, but chasing after a hungry wolf wasn't something he wanted to do right now.

"Might be sick," Slocum said. "It was going after its prey from upwind, so the cattle could smell it coming."

"Don't let that worry you none," Tewksbury said. "Huntin's easy here and even the wolves aren't too bright. Don't have to be."

Slocum shoved his rifle back into its scabbard. He didn't understand what was going on around here. Tewksbury couldn't make a living off cattle, and yet the wolves were so bold they didn't care if they were scented before they attacked. Everything was mixed up.

"We might have more cattle to deal with, if you still want to drive 'em to market fer me."

"How's that?"

"Let's skcdaddle on back to the house," Tewksbury said. "Don't look like two-legged wolves are after any of these beeves."

Slocum wondered at the man's sudden loss of interest in cattle he had been so keen on protecting before. The wolf would have brought down one cow at the most and still might. But this had been important enough to leave the Daggs brothers after a big business deal was closed. Now Tewksbury had to return to the house.

Slocum rode in silence, hardly listening to the man chattering away like a magpie. As they reached the double-rutted road leading to the ranch house, Slocum drew rein and cocked his head to one side.

"What's up, Slocum?"

"Listen. Cattle and lots of them. What's going on?"

Tewksbury grinned and said, "Caleb and the boys've been busy tonight. And Graham's got maybe a hundred head fewer in his herd to worry over."

Slocum stared at him in amazement. Tewksbury had wanted him away while his son and hired hands were out rustling a neighbor's cattle, because Slocum would object.

"What's wrong, Slocum? You ain't squeamish 'bout liberatin' a few of Graham's cows, are you?"

"I'll take the beeves owed me and be moving on at first

light," Slocum said. "And I want only the cattle with the Circle T brand."

Tewksbury laughed and said, "Hell, boy, by dawn that'll be all them beeves!"

Slocum knew it was time to clear out.

8

"We 'found' damn near eighty head of cattle, Pa," Caleb Tewksbury said proudly. Slocum tried to ignore the man's glee and couldn't. He wasn't above a little rustling himself, but the Tewksburys and Graham had it all wrong. Stealing from someone who knew you were responsible was well nigh loco.

"Run the brands quick-like," Tewksbury said. "I don't want none of them beeves lookin' like they been grazin' on Graham grass. You hear me?"

"I do, Pa. I already got an iron heatin'. You want to help, Slocum?"

"I don't think so," Slocum said.

"Slocum here's gettin' a little squeamish. He wants his cows so he can be on the trail. Make sure they're all our brands," Tewksbury said.

"Not a run brand, either," Slocum said harshly. "Waltzing into Prescott with stolen cattle for sale is a sure way to get my neck stretched."

"The sheriff's not a bad sort," Tewksbury said, "but he is gettin' tired of dealin' with Graham."

"Those cattle up in the valley," Slocum said. "I'll cut out my due from those."

"Suit yerself, Slocum," Tewksbury said. He stretched

74

and yawned mightily. "I need to get some sleep. But I'm powerful hungry. Where's Lydia?"

"Ain't seen her, Pa," Caleb said. "She must be in bed already."

Slocum wondered how much of the illegal dealings Lydia knew about. She was no fool, but Tewksbury could be mighty sly and obviously kept a great deal from her. Slocum smiled as he thought of the times he had spent with Lydia. Such furtiveness must be inherited, because she had managed to keep her affairs secret from her father. At least Slocum hoped she had. He had the feeling that Tewksbury would be quick to use that shotgun of his on anyone sniffing around his daughter.

After he tended his mare, Slocum walked to the bunkhouse. He could hardly keep his eyes open but knew he had to be up in an hour or two and hit the trail. If he lingered, he might never get out of the Tonto Basin. He dropped flat on his back, staring up at the bunkhouse ceiling. He was drifting off to sleep when the door was flung open and banged hard against the wall.

Slocum's reactions were slowed by exhaustion, but he still had his six-shooter out, cocked and pointed at the man standing in the door.

"What is it, Caleb?"

"She's not here, Slocum. She's gone. Lydia's nowhere to be found."

"Well, she's not here, either," Slocum said, lowering the hammer and tucking his Colt away in its holster.

"Pa wants to see you right now, Slocum. Please."

Slocum growled like a bear as he sat up. It took him a few minutes to get his boots back on and his gunbelt slung. By the time he reached the ranch house, he was fuming mad.

His anger died when he saw Tewksbury's face. The man was pale under his weathered skin and his hand shook as he lifted a tin cup and drank from it.

"She's gone, Slocum. They got her. That son of a bitch Graham's got her."

"How do you know that?" Slocum asked. He pulled up a chair and sank onto it. Every line on Tewksbury's leathery face showed concern. Not for the first time Slocum wondered if the man was playing him for a fool. If he was this time, he was doing a great job.

"She's always here. Where else'd she go?"

"There's no telling," Slocum said. "Maybe her horse ran off and she went after it?"

"Star's still in the corral, but another horse is missing— one that you just broke. Ain't no reason fer her to take it and leave Star."

"I'll scout around," Slocum said. "You stay here. I've had more than enough of your tall tales for one night."

"The others, those was mostly made up, Slocum, but not this. I'd never josh around 'bout Lydia like this."

Slocum had to believe him. Stride long, he went to the corral behind the barn and quickly located Star. The other horses in the corral had been saddle broke before Slocum showed up. They had put one newly broke horse in with the others to get it used to the notion of men carrying saddles and tack around it. The other four he had broken were in another corral. Slocum climbed to the top rail and peered at them. All were there. The only horse missing was the new one from this pen.

He jumped to the ground and walked around the gate hunting for Lydia's distinctively small boot print. He didn't find it, but there were several larger, deeper ones both outside and just inside the corral. Dropping to his knees, he fumbled out a lucifer and lit it to better examine the prints. The flickering light revealed that at least three men had recently entered the corral. Since Caleb had the rest of the hands from the Circle T with him on his rustling expedition, that didn't leave a whole lot to the imagination.

Slocum followed what he thought was the right set of hoofprints to the far side of the barn. When he saw the small prints here, he sat heavily and stared. It took a few minutes for him to reconstruct what must have happened. Three men brought the newly saddle-broken horse around.

Three others had escorted Lydia from the house and held her here until she mounted. Then they rode off. The best he could tell, seven horses had left but there was no way to tell how many had ridden onto the Circle T.

"They got her, don't they?"

Slocum looked up at Tewksbury.

"They rode that way," Slocum said, pointing north. "We might have just missed them as we returned, though they look to be angling away."

"Toward Graham's spread."

"They might have taken her a couple hours ago but not longer than that," Slocum said.

"I'll get Caleb and the others and go fetch her. That sidewinder's not keepin' my little girl!"

"Hold on, Tewksbury. You go barging onto Graham's land and he will gun you down. That might be what he intends. Lydia might be bait to get you onto his property so he'll have some standing with the law." This sounded hollow even to Slocum. Graham and Tewksbury weren't that subtle, and laying ambushes for each other was out of the question. They were like two elk in rut, banging antlers in all-out fighting, and nothing less than death would end the battle.

"I ain't lettin' her rot there. There's no tellin' what horrible thing Graham would do to her!"

"How many men does Graham have? Including Murphy and the one that probably ran off after I shot him."

"A dozen, maybe more. And there's Mrs. Graham."

Slocum looked sharply at Tewksbury. Why mention Graham's wife at all?

"I gotta go, Slocum."

"Stay here, for a while. I'll scout around and see if there might not be a way of getting Lydia away without swapping a lot of lead."

"I want to kill him!"

"Fine, kill him, but is his life more important to you than your daughter's?"

"No, but Graham—"

"If I'm not back by sundown, do whatever you want." Slocum forestalled more argument by holding up his hand. "Think about it. If Graham wanted Lydia dead, he could have shot her here. Or if he wanted to rape her, there was plenty of opportunity here for that, too. I suspect he wants to hold her hostage, probably to get his cattle back."

"He can't have 'em!"

"Shut up," Slocum said coldly. "If I have to, I'll trade him this entire damned ranch for Lydia being released unharmed."

"No, yes, I see what yer gettin' at, Slocum, and yer right."

"Bring me a couple horses. I'll take my mare along, but I want a pair of rested horses, in case they're needed for a quick getaway."

"Git her back safe and sound," Tewksbury said. "And I don't care if you plug Graham."

Slocum wondered how being dead and burning in hell could be any worse than this.

Sneaking into the Graham ranch would be hard. Slocum rode to the edge of a stock tank and looked across it to the Graham ranch house. More than a dozen men bustled about doing their chores. Another pair were posted as sentries near the house's front door, but they weren't up to the job. They sat together, passing a cigarette back and forth between them and feeling comfortable in the middle of Graham's little empire.

Slocum dismounted and let his three horses have their fill before leading them away to a nearby wooded area. From here it was a half mile to the house with nothing but level grassland. Even if he got Lydia out of the house, returning to the horses would be difficult. And in the middle of the day it would be impossible. Slocum chafed at any delay, since he had gotten the promise from Tewksbury to wait only until dark. Slocum had no doubt the rancher would come galloping down the road, shotgun blazing. Men would die. Probably Tewksbury but also his daughter.

This wasn't Slocum's fight, but he felt obligated to get Lydia out of this jam. He had saved her before from the Apaches, and doing it again from a white man shouldn't be as hard. But it was.

Patience had always been a virtue that worked in Slocum's favor. Rather than rush in like Tewksbury would do, Slocum sat, watched and guessed what Graham might do. After the noon meal, he saw a small army of men ride out. Judging from the way they rode, they were going out to tend a herd and round up strays. They might even be working on fences, though he saw none of them with wire or equipment.

"Time to do something other than sit on my butt," Slocum said, brushing himself off. He left the horse he had ridden and took the two fresh mounts, knowing speed might be his savior getting away from the Graham house. The two guards napped in the afternoon heat and didn't see Slocum riding up until he was almost on top of them. One stirred and rubbed his eyes.

"Got a message for the boss. Is Mr. Graham inside?" Slocum saw that this easy familiarity lulled the guards. One snored loudly, and the one who had stirred made a vague gesture toward the front door.

"He's inside? Good, thanks." Slocum waved to the man and looped the reins of the horses through a ring set on a post. He hesitated at the last step before going onto the porch, to be certain the guard wasn't going to shoot him in the back. The man snored as loudly as his partner.

Slocum went to the door, tested the latch and then opened it slowly to avoid any creaking of the hinges. The day was warm outside, but the interior of the house was cool and inviting. With a smooth motion, Slocum slid his six-gun from the holster and looked around for Tom Graham. He had taken only two steps into the house when a door opened.

"Freeze," Slocum said, aiming the six-shooter directly at Graham. The rancher took a step back, but when Slocum cocked the pistol he did as he was told.

"Didn't think I'd see you again. You're goin' be pushin' up daisies, comin' here like this."

"I came for Lydia Tewksbury," Slocum said. Graham's eyebrows arched and he started to say something but no words came out. The reaction puzzled Slocum. "Where is she?"

"Back there," Graham said. "But she's not goin' nowhere."

"Where's your wife?" Again Slocum was baffled at the rancher's expression.

"Gone for the day. Won't be back until late tonight." Graham summoned up his courage and said more belligerently, "You givin' me back my beeves? The ones you stole last night."

"No matter what rustling went on," Slocum said, "that's no excuse to kidnap a young woman like that."

"Kidnap?" Graham laughed harshly. "Call it what you will. I want my cattle back."

"I'll see that Tewksbury returns them. You can send a couple cowboys to the road in front of his spread tomorrow at dawn. The cattle will be waiting—if Lydia's not been hurt."

"She's fit as a fiddle," Graham said. Again Slocum wondered at the rancher's attitude.

"Come on out into the room," Slocum said, "and get down on your knees." Slocum waited for Graham to obey, then looked into the room beyond. Lydia sat on the bed, calm as could be. She looked up when he poked his head in.

"John!"

"Come on. I'm getting you out of here. Your pa's been worried sick when he found you were missing."

"But *you* came to fetch me," she said. "You're so brave!" She threw her arms around his neck and kissed him. Slocum pushed her away in time to turn and get Graham back into his sights. The man had begun edging toward the door to the porch.

"Don't make me cut you down," Slocum said. "If you don't like the deal, I can renegotiate it right now. With a slug."

"Go on, get out of here," Graham said.

"You look kinda nice down on your knees like that, Mr. Graham," Lydia said. "In fact, that's where you ought to be all the time."

"Get going," Slocum said, pushing her toward the door. "I might have to shoot him if he tries to call out to a pair of guards posted outside."

"You didn't kill them?" Graham snarled like a cougar. "I'll skin them both alive lettin' you sneak up on me like this."

Slocum took two quick steps and swung his pistol, landing the hard steel barrel on the side of Graham's head. He fell heavily to the floor and lay still.

"John, you didn't have to—"

"Come on, Lydia. I had to keep him quiet. And you don't make a sound when we get outside. Get on your horse and ride out slowly. If you do anything to draw attention, there'll be a whole passel of men dying."

"I wouldn't want one of them to be you, John. I wouldn't."

"Don't look at the guards. Don't make any sudden noise," Slocum said. His hand twitched as he longed to turn his six-shooter on the two sleeping guards and plug them. He and Lydia would have their backs to the men for some time as they went to the horses and rode away.

"I'm nervous, John," she said.

"Your horse is saddled and ready." Slocum was glad he had switched his saddle to the fresh horse before riding in. He waited a moment, to be sure Lydia got her seat, before he swung into the saddle. Neither of the guards stirred. Slocum inclined his head in the direction of the wooded patch where he had left the other horse. It might be pay enough for getting Lydia free, but losing even one horse he didn't have to rankled.

"We made it," the woman said with a deep sigh.

The words were hardly out of her mouth when Tom Graham stumbled from the house, yelling for his men.

"Ride!" Slocum called. "Hard!"

Heads down, they galloped away, but the hail of bullets Slocum expected never came. He did hear sounds that told him Graham and his sleepy guards were saddling up to come after them.

"My horse is tiring fast, John," Lydia told him when they were almost at the wooded area where the other horse cropped at grass. It looked up curiously as Slocum slowed, reached down and scooped up the reins. A quick tug got the horse moving reluctantly from its mid-afternoon repast.

"Here," Slocum said, tossing the reins to her. "Ride as hard as you can until the horse you're on starts to stumble. Switch to this horse. It's all rested. Get on back to your pa as fast as you can and talk him out of doing anything dumb."

"What might that be?"

"He was going to launch an attack on Graham and his men. Didn't matter he would be outnumbered three to one. I made him promise to hold off until sundown, but if I know him, he's already on the road with that shotgun just itching to fire it into Graham's face."

"He can't do that!"

"More'n him would get killed. Your brother and whatever hands he can talk into it would be in shallow graves before sunrise, too."

"If Tom even thought to bury them," Lydia said angrily.

"I'll decoy them away."

"Let me change horses now. You take mine. Leaving a trail with two horses is more likely to draw them than just yours."

He saw how lathered her horse was and agreed. Lydia expertly moved the saddle to the rested horse and mounted. Slocum was getting antsy about how close Graham and his boys would be by now. Shooting it out with three men would be hard, and Graham might have rounded up a few more. Getting buffaloed in his own house and having his hostage snatched from under his nose was an affront to his honor he wasn't likely to let go unavenged.

"Go on, ride like you mean it," Slocum said, but Lydia

brought her horse close to his, leaned over and gave him a quick, fleeting kiss on the lips.

"Thank you," she whispered, then put her heels to her horse and raced away.

Slocum waited until she disappeared down a ravine before turning at an angle and heading for higher ground to lead Graham and his posse away. He had barely reached the ridge when he spotted Graham and four men behind. They didn't see him because they were too intent on studying the tracks in the ground. Graham's tracker had found the hoofprints and pointed uphill. As he did, he spotted Slocum.

Slocum waited long enough for all the men to see him, then trotted down the far side of the hill, cut sharply to go into a rocky area, cut off at another angle and then waited behind a grassy knoll, heart hammering as he heard them approaching. Graham argued with his tracker over where Slocum had gone.

"Lit out, makin' a beeline for the west," Graham said.

"He's tryin' to confuse us," the tracker said. Slocum swore under his breath. The man must be part Indian the way he had picked up on the numerous cutbacks and changes in direction across the rocky stretch.

"He's only confusin' you," Graham said. "After him. West!"

The tracker grumbled but obeyed. Slocum heaved a sigh of relief at not having to shoot it out with five armed and angry men. After a decent time, he turned south toward the Tewksbury spread and made as good time as he could. Now more than ever he had to take his due and leave the Tonto Basin. Too much hatred had built up for there to be anything but a bloodbath.

9

"Where's your pa?" Slocum felt as if he had been punched in the gut. He had evaded Graham and his men, returned to the ranch and expected to see Tewksbury waiting for him. The man had obviously ignored the promise not to go after Graham until sundown. Slocum pulled his hat brim down and squinted into the sun. There was a good hour of daylight left, and Tewksbury had jumped the gun.

"I'm worried about him, John," Lydia said. "He might be getting himself into a world of woe if—"

Slocum caught movement out of the corner of his eye, dug his toes into the ground for traction and dived forward. His arms circled the woman's slender waist and his shoulder smashed into her belly. He heard the wind gusting from her lungs as he carried her backward out of the path of a bullet meant to kill her. They landed in a pile, Lydia kicking feebly and gasping for breath.

"Stay down," he said needlessly. She wasn't going to do anything until she sucked in enough air to fill her lungs again. He rolled, dragged out his six-gun and fired. Dust kicked up around him, and more than one bullet ricocheted off a buried rock. Slocum sat up and fanned the hammer on his pistol, getting off five more shots faster than the sniper shooting at him could chamber new rounds in his rifle.

Slocum doubted any of his bullets hit the man, but wood splintered near the man's face and drove him back around the house. Slocum jammed his six-shooter into his holster, rolled back, grabbed Lydia by the wrist and pulled her to her feet. The woman stumbled and fell to her knees, still gasping.

"If you don't run for the barn, you're dead," he whispered hotly in her ear. "Do you hear me?"

"Y-yes," she got out. Slocum had to hand it to Lydia. She was a fighter. In spite of her lack of air, she kept moving. Slocum followed behind, providing a shield for her. He tried to get to his horse and the rifle there, but the sniper at the side of the house wasn't going to let that happen.

Slocum shoved Lydia forward when they got close enough to the barn, so she staggered inside and fell heavily into a pile of straw.

"Stay down," he ordered.

"C-can't do much," she got out. "R-rifle back th-there." She pointed toward the rear of the barn. Slocum had already started in that direction. He threw open an equipment box and saw a small-caliber varmint rifle, good for rats and rabbits but not much else. It was still better than the empty Colt Navy in his holster, so he grabbed the rifle and a box of shells which he shoved into his coat pocket.

"It's only a single-shot rifle," Slocum called to her, "so I won't be able to stop them all if they rush us."

"Is there another one? I'm still a bit shaky after you knocked me down, but I can shoot."

"This is the only rifle," Slocum said. He considered his chances of getting to his horse again and knew he didn't stand two hoots in hell of making it. A second rifle barrel poked around the side of the house.

"I see three of them," Lydia said. "All of them are behind the house. They must have just ridden in."

"You recognize them?"

"They must be Graham's men." Lydia sounded dubious about this, but that wasn't what Slocum had meant.

"You see Graham?"

"No!"

Again her response puzzled him. She seemed outraged that he would think Graham might come to kill her—as exasperated as she was with her father for going after Graham. Slocum slid a small shell into the rifle and slammed shut the bolt. The distance made his marksmanship a joke. The bullet from such a small-caliber rifle had too short a range to matter much. Then he got his chance. One man poked his head around the house, waited, then ducked back. Slocum knew the gunmen argued over whether Slocum was out of ammo, and this brief act of foolish defiance had proven it to at least two of the men.

Slocum fell to the ground and aimed carefully, waiting for the right instant to fire. Two gunmen came running around the corner, firing their rifles as they came. Running and shooting sent their lead flying about wildly. Slocum's trigger finger drew back slowly and the tiny *pop!* surprised him. The rifle had a lighter pull than he'd expected.

One of the riflemen stumbled and fell, screaming as he clawed at his leg.

"I been shot. He blowed my damn leg off!"

Slocum methodically opened the rifle, ejected the spent casing and put in a new shell. He fired as the man rose up and pointed at his leg. This slug put a hole in the man's hat—he didn't even notice it. Slocum got a third shot off before the man's partner skidded to a halt, reversed course and grabbed his friend to drag him to cover. Slocum shot at the good Samaritan but missed. His next round was a dud.

"The ammunition's been in that box for a year," Lydia said, coming up beside him. She peered around the barn door at their attackers. "Can you hold them off?"

"For a while," Slocum said. He wondered how long it would take the men—three?—to figure out they faced only one rifle, and a small-bore one, to boot?

"What should we do?"

"Any chance of getting out back to the corral? If you can get your horse, you can get away. I'll hold them off while you make a break."

"You do that a lot, don't you, John?"

He looked at her and had to grin.

"Reckon so. You get going. It's not going to take them long to decide a Mexican standoff's not what they want."

"After you shot one of them, you think they'll still make a frontal attack?"

"I would."

"But you're brave. Those men aren't."

Slocum knew she was trying to compliment him, but it had the opposite effect. Staying to take potshots at well-armed men when all he had was a varmint rifle was more stupid than brave, but he saw no other way to be sure Lydia got away. He hadn't ridden into the middle of Graham's stronghold to rescue Lydia, only to have her snatched away under his nose.

He squeezed off a shot that took out a window in the house. The bullet wasn't wasted, though, since the cascade of glass chased a sniper away from what might have been a dangerous position for Slocum.

"Hurry, John. Don't stay too long," Lydia said. She paused; then he heard her running to the rear of the barn and going to the corral. He fired again and the slug went wide. He tried to figure windage or how the sights were off, but finally decided that the ammunition was bad. He'd be lucky if the rifle didn't blow up in his face.

He fumbled out another shell and felt that there were only a few cartridges left from the box. Slocum took a quick shot and got to his feet, preparing to follow Lydia. He turned and ran smack into the woman. Lydia stood behind him, eyes wide and filled with tears.

"Th-they took Star."

He swung around her and glanced out the rear door. His heart sank. Graham's men had stolen all the horses in the corral, including Lydia's precious Star. His mind raced.

"Get up into the loft," he told her. "Stay low. Hide until—"

"Star!" Lydia grabbed his arm and jerked hard enough

to swing him around. "They took him. How could Graham do such a terrible thing?"

"They'll do more than that if you don't do as I say," Slocum told her. "Get up there. Now!" The snap in his voice caused her to jump. She stared at him with wide eyes and tried to talk. Words refused to come out. He pushed her toward the ladder leading to the loft, then whirled about and fired his rifle as one of Graham's men burst through the open door. The tiny *pop!* didn't sound like much, but the man stopped in his tracks, looked down stupidly at his chest and then fell like a huge redwood sawed through the base.

"Damn," Slocum said, seeing that he had shot the man straight through the heart. It had been more luck than skill. But he wasted no time rushing to the man's side and grabbing his rifle. With a more powerful weapon, he started a measured, accurate fire that winged two of the men trying to rush the front of the barn.

They got the hint and shouted at each other to retreat. Slocum came up empty and threw the rifle aside. He rolled over the man he had shot through the heart and drew his six-shooter. Two more shots was all it took before he heard the thunder of hooves from behind the Tewksbury house. Graham's henchmen had finally called it quits.

"What do you see from up there?"

"I . . . Five men, all riding like somebody set fire to their tails. I don't see Star. None of them's riding Star!"

"All the horses were stolen earlier," Slocum said. "We happened onto the last of the horse thieves, and they thought they could kill us."

"Tom'd never do that," Lydia said in a voice almost too low for Slocum to hear. Almost.

Slocum climbed the ladder to the hayloft and went to stand beside Lydia. She hung out the hayloft door as she tried to spot her horse.

"You sound mighty friendly with Graham," he said. "What's going on between you?"

"Between us? Nothing," she said too quickly for it to be the truth.

"You and him lovers?"

"What if we are? Does that change anything between us?"

"I risked my life to save you. Your pa doesn't know, does he?"

"No," she said. "But I swear, John, it's all over between me and Tom Graham now. How could he do such a thing!"

"He might have actually kidnapped you because he was angry at your pa for rustling a hundred head of cattle."

"Pa did that?"

"He sent Caleb and a few cowboys out to do it. Caleb bragged on it to me."

"He can be such a fool," Lydia said sadly, shaking her head. The sunlight caught her auburn hair and turned it to a red-gold that brought a catch to Slocum's throat. Lydia Tewksbury was nothing if not lovely, but she was as twisted as a gnarly old oak—just like the rest of her family.

"I don't know where your father and brother got off to, but I suspect they decided to use my sneaking around to rescue you as a diversion for more devilment."

"Why, I might have been killed!"

Slocum said nothing. The same idea had occurred to him. Tewksbury hated Graham so much he was willing to sacrifice his own daughter to get even with the other rancher.

"John," Lydia said, turning to him. "You've got to get him back."

For a moment Slocum wasn't sure who she meant. Then it hit him that she wasn't talking about either her father or brother. And she certainly didn't mean Tom Graham. She thought more of her horse than she did any human.

Any human, including John Slocum.

"I'm clearing out," he told her. "I should have done this the minute I laid eyes on you."

"That wasn't all that got laid, was it, John?" she said. She moved closer and ran her fingers up and through his hair, bringing his face down to hers for a big, wet kiss. "I can reward you, John. I can give you everything a man could ever want."

"Like you did Graham?"

She jerked away as if he had burned her with a branding iron.

"That was a cruel thing to say. I'm done with him! He was only using me and I cared for him."

"You pa mentioned Graham was married," Slocum said. "You knew that, didn't you?"

"He doesn't love her. They . . . they never sleep together anymore. He wants to divorce her, but that's mighty hard to do out here, a hundred miles from the nearest judge."

Slocum had heard worse, but Lydia hadn't seemed the sort of woman to fall for a story like that.

"I'll stay until your pa gets back," he said. "The way Graham's men lit out of here, though, I don't think there's going to be any more trouble."

"I want Star back, John. Please. You got him once before. Do it again." She read the answer in his expression. She clung to him. "Please, I love that horse more than anything in the whole world." She looked up, her brown eyes brimming with tears. "Even more than I love you," she said.

"That might be the first honest thing you've said," Slocum declared.

"I'll make it worth your while. Those horses they stole. You can have all of them and the cattle Pa promised for breaking the mustangs."

"They're not yours to give away."

"Papa owes me," she said, a hint of steel coming into her words. "He'll give them to you."

"Ten horses plus a hundred head of cattle," Slocum said.

Lydia thought it over a moment and then nodded, her hair flying about her face in wild disarray. In spite of himself, Slocum saw her and wanted her. Maybe the moment of vulnerability and honesty convinced him to do such a foolish thing—or it might have been greed. He wanted to get the hell out of the Tonto Basin with his hide intact, but it would be doubly good if he got away with enough in the way of wealth on the hoof to make everything he had gone through worthwhile.

"Go now, John, catch up with them and get Star back for me. I'll be all right here."

"We'll write up a contract," he said. "Put everything in writing we just agreed on."

"I understand," she said. They dropped down the ladder and went to the house, where Lydia found ink and a sheet of clean paper. It took her a few minutes to put everything down, and even longer for Slocum to go over it, crossing out parts and changing others.

"Sign it," he said.

"This makes it legal," she said, attaching her signature with a flourish. She thrust out her hand. "Shake on it. My word's my bond, too."

He shook and she pulled him close and gave him another kiss.

"Better than just a handshake," she said. "Bring back Star and even more will be yours."

Slocum didn't give her an answer, because it would have been too sarcastic. He rummaged through a cabinet near the door and found a box of shells for his rifle. He tucked them into his coat pocket and left without so much as a backward look at the woman. He was fed up with the Tewksburys and their ways.

He swung into the saddle, then fumbled around in his saddlebags for the fixings to reload his Colt. Not taking the time to do it while he sat still, he let the horse begin walking as he worked. This proved clumsier, but Slocum wanted to get this chore over and done with as quick as possible.

He retraced the path to the Graham ranch and reached there two hours after sundown. From the same spot in the woods where he had spied on Graham before, he took in the activity around the house. For a place where stolen horses had been put into the corral behind the barn, the entire area seemed curiously quiet.

Slocum rode straight for the corral and looked over the horses and the brands on their hips. All had been stolen from Tewksbury. And Star had been placed in his own corral some distance away. He took care of Lydia's horse first, dropping a lariat around the horse's neck and leading it from the smaller corral. The horse nickered and pressed its head against him.

"We're getting to be real buddies, aren't we?" Slocum patted the horse's neck and gentled it. Stealing a horse was about the lowest thing a man could do, and Graham had done it. Slocum wasn't sure of the provocation, but it was still horse stealing. If Graham had a gripe, he should come out and say so. If it meant gunplay, so be it. From everything he had seen, Tewksbury wasn't the kind to turn and run if Graham demanded a showdown.

Slocum led Star back to the other corral, then began lacing their bridles together so he could lead the remuda out without worrying about strays giving him away.

He mounted and got the string of horses moving, but Slocum grew increasingly uneasy as he rode from the Graham ranch. He had expected at least one challenge, but even the sleepy guards Graham had posted before were missing. A quick look toward the bunkhouse showed it was dark and empty. Slocum rode back to the woods and fastened the lead rope to a tree before intently studying the ranch house again.

Lydia had wanted her horse back, and Slocum had rescued Star one more, last, time. In addition, he had most of the horses that had been stolen from the Tewksbury corral. They were his now, they and a hundred head of cattle. The contract riding in his pocket assured him of that.

"Ought to take the horses, forget the cattle and clear out," Slocum said to himself, but he wasn't going to steal Lydia's horse. He had promised to return Star, and he would. When he got back, he might as well collect his herd of cattle, too.

But the eerie quiet from Graham's house stopped Slocum from riding out immediately. He had been on enough raids to know how men acted afterward. A successful raid meant passing a whiskey bottle around and bragging on how brave and clever they all were, each trying to top the next in tall tales. And if the raid had failed, the whiskey was still passed around, but blame was dished out, too. Those who had died were the usual scapegoats.

But in either case, the men returned to their camp. Slocum saw nothing stirring at the Graham ranch.

Cursing himself as a fool, he rode straight into the yard in front of the house.

"Graham!" he called. "Come on out. We got to talk."

He would settle things between Graham and Tewksbury once and for all.

"Graham?"

When he heard no answer—or even the scurrying of men running for cover—he dismounted and went up the steps to the porch. He opened the door and peered into the darkened parlor.

"Graham?"

Slocum took a whiff of the air and smelled gunpowder. He cocked his drawn Colt, stepped into Graham's house and immediately swung the muzzle around to point at Tom Graham.

There wasn't any call to do this. Graham was sprawled in a chair, arms flopped out on either side. A bullet hole in the middle of his forehead gave mute testimony to how dead he was.

10

"Comes as a whale of a surprise to me, Slocum," John Tewksbury said, shaking his head. "Don't know who done it. Wish I had, but it wasn't me. Not Caleb or any of my boys, either." Tewksbury canted his head to one side and stared hard at Slocum. "You do believe me, don't you?"

"Who else hated Graham enough to shoot him in the face?" Slocum asked.

"Hell, that could be damn near anyone else in the Basin. Graham never went out of his way to make friends."

"This makes your life here a lot easier, doesn't it?"

"Cain't say it don't," Tewksbury said.

"You aren't accusing Papa of being a murderer, are you?" Lydia stared at him in disbelief. "Even if he did kill Tom, what difference does it make?"

"Graham wasn't wearing a gun," Slocum said. "I didn't even see one near him. Whoever killed him murdered an unarmed man."

"Happens," Caleb said, as if it had taken this long for him to understand what was going on. "Could have been any of his men. Murphy's a bad apple. You know that first-hand, Slocum."

Slocum ignored the young man and watched his father closely. He couldn't decide if Tewksbury was responsible.

"Where were you and the rest? Lydia and I got here right after Graham's men stole the horses. You were supposed to wait until sundown before hitting the trail."

"I was going to wait, Slocum, I was. But gettin' ready to go on in and shoot up Graham's place wasn't part of our deal. The instant that ole sun dipped b'low the horizon, I was goin' to show him what for."

"It put your daughter's life in danger."

"Wouldn't have if Graham hadn't been such a skunk. Stealin' my horses like that! He was a thief and a killer!"

"I got the horses back," Slocum said. "I'll cut out my cattle in the morning and be out of here. There's nothing I can do here."

"Please, John, stay awhile longer," pleaded Lydia. "It . . . it's nice having you around here."

Slocum started to tell Lydia he wasn't going to be her substitute for Tom Graham, but he held his tongue. Graham was dead, and there was no point in further inflaming Tewksbury. The man was crazy enough to burn down Graham's house and kill any of his men he happened on, simply because they had worked for Graham.

"Can't say it's been entirely pleasant here," Slocum said. "I'll leave you folks to your gloating."

"Damn right, Slocum," cried Tewksbury. "Not every day the biggest thorn in your paw gets plucked out!"

Slocum left, stepping into the cool night air. The stars stretched from one side of the sky to the other, a thick band almost overhead, giving enough light to read by. It was hard to believe such peace arched over the turmoil through the Tonto Basin. Slocum doubted Graham's murder would end it. In spite of what Tewksbury said, Graham had friends who would avenge his death. And there were relatives. Tewksbury had made a point of mentioning that when Slocum first rode onto the Circle T.

"John?"

"You take care of Star?" Slocum asked. He didn't want to have anything more to do with Lydia, but there was an undeniable attraction. She was about the prettiest woman he had come across in years, but then a coral snake was mighty pretty, too.

"I don't want to talk about the horse, John. Are you sure that Tom was murdered?"

"He didn't shoot himself in the forehead like that, then hide the six-shooter."

"It could have been Murphy, like Caleb said. Or any of his men. He treated them badly."

"But he didn't treat you bad?"

"Please, he was a strong man. A rich, powerful man and he had a certain animal attraction I was too weak to resist."

Slocum started walking and Lydia fell into step beside him.

"You wouldn't understand, John," she said. "I got mighty lonely, and he was good to me."

"To the point of stealing your horse."

"I think that might have been Tom's way of trying to convince me to leave Papa and go live with him."

"He was married. What were you going to do, live in the barn so he could sneak out from his home and wife?"

"John," she said in exasperation. "You *really* don't understand."

"Reckon that's right. I don't understand and don't much want to."

"It's all over now."

The words weren't out of her mouth when the air filled with lead. For an instant, Slocum wasn't sure what was going on; then he realized they were the targets. He dived flat on the ground, fumbling to get his six-shooter drawn. He never got a chance to shoot.

A rider galloped up to the front of the house, not seeing either Slocum or Lydia in the yard.

"Tewksbury, you mangy son of a bitch! You kilt him. I'll see you in hell for what you did!"

A few more rounds from the rider's six-shooter took out what windows remained in the house; then the rider took off at a gallop.

Slocum sat up and aimed his pistol at the dark form now rapidly vanishing.

"Who was that?" Slocum asked.

"Trouble," Lydia said, "Big trouble. That was 'Old Man' Matt Blevins. He and Tom were thicker than thieves."

"Sounds like he had more friends than you or your pa let on."

Slocum took no satisfaction in being right about the re-action to Graham's murder. He got up and dusted himself off. Lydia remained on the ground, hand extended for him to help her up. He considered for a moment, then manners dictated that he pull her to her feet.

"You git a shot at him, Slocum?" Tewksbury and Caleb came out, clutching their shotguns.

"All I did was see what direction he rode," Slocum said, "so I can ride in the other."

"Never pegged you fer a coward," Tewksbury said. "Reckon I don't much blame you, though. His kid's a stone killer."

"So?"

"So Andy's likely to be back, if Matt's kickin' up a fuss like this."

"Back from where?"

"You might have heard of him," Lydia said, looking flushed. Slocum wondered at her excitement.

"Andy Blevins? Nope."

"Not Blevins. Andy Cooper, from Texas. He was down San Antonio way and got into trouble with the law, so he changed his name for all the good that did him."

"He shot a man in the back," Slocum said, going cold all over. His hand rested on the ebony handle of his six-shooter.

"See? He's famous. You do know of him," Tewksbury said.

"No," Slocum said slowly. "I don't know of him. I know him. And we have a score to settle."

"No question about it," Slocum said, dismounting. He swung the mare's reins around the ring in the post. "That's Cooper."

"What's your beef with him, Slocum?" Tewksbury asked. "I never seen a man turn so cold as you did when you found out Andy Cooper was here in the Basin."

"That man he shot in the back?"

"Down in San Antone? What of him?"

"He was my partner. We'd ridden together for close to six months when he got into a poker game with Cooper. My friend won and Cooper held him up, then shot him in the back. I tried to track him down but ran into a Texas Ranger that didn't take kindly to anyone cutting in on his reward. By the time I got away from the Ranger, Cooper was gone."

"Rangers kin be like that," Tewksbury said, stroking his chin. "So you still leavin' or you stayin' awhile longer?"

"I want Cooper," Slocum said.

"Well, you kin stay here, but you got to pay to feed yer horses and all them cattle you claimed as yers."

Slocum wondered if he wouldn't be serving humanity by putting a bullet into Tewksbury and then going after Cooper.

"I'll pay you in cattle," he said.

"Nope, cain't do that. We got the sheep comin' in. Truth is, that there Basque shepherd's already here. The Daggs boys tole me he's set up northwest of here on some un-grazed pastureland."

"Land adjoining Graham's?"

"A goodly hunk of my land's that way," Tewksbury said with some contempt. "Might be I kin annex a bit more of Graham's pasture when you kill Cooper. Blevins ain't gonna care none, either, since I'm gonna take care of him myself."

"Pa, Pa!" Caleb Tewksbury came riding up, looking flustered.

Seeing him, Slocum heaved a deep sigh. There was never anything but bad news on the Circle T.

"What is it, boy?"

"Pa, Blevins and his men are killin' the sheep. They're stampedin' 'em and killin' 'em and—"

"Calm down," Tewksbury said. "You tell me what happened. Don't stammer none, Caleb, don't you dare. Time's important."

"Yes, sir, time's awastin'," Caleb said, sliding from the saddle and almost falling. "Been ridin' too hard. But Old Man Blevins and Andy Cooper started shootin' up the herd."

"Flock," Slocum corrected mechanically. "Cooper was there?"

"Bold as brass," Caleb said.

"I'll ride with you," Slocum said, grabbing his mare's reins. He saw a chance to end this right away. Cooper was a coward, more intent on shooting another in the back than on facing someone who might plug him. Slocum didn't much care which way Cooper was facing when he shot him, but he hoped it was face to face. He wanted to see Cooper crawl before he emptied his six-shooter into his belly.

Slocum rode with Caleb on one side and Tewksbury on the other. Both men chattered away endlessly, getting on Slocum's nerves. They arrived at the pastureland eventually and let Slocum get a good view of what it meant for sheep to be let loose on cattle grazing land. It looked as if there had been a snowstorm, with a thousand or more of the woollies bent low and pulling up the grass as they grazed.

"Where's Cooper?" Slocum asked Caleb. The young man pointed to the eastern side of the pasture.

"Blevins is with him, too," Caleb said.

Slocum didn't care. If Matt Blevins tried to stop him from getting to Cooper, he would die. It was going to end here. Now.

"Slocum, slow down. Let us keep up with you!" Tewksbury and his son trotted along behind, but Slocum wasn't going to slow down. He had reached the edge of the flock when he heard gunfire. Unlike cattle, the sheep showed little upset at the shots fired. Slocum tried to identify the types of weapons discharged. One sounded like a six-shooter and another a rifle. But the third gun carried a curious sound to it unlike anything he had ever heard. He urged the mare to even more speed as he reached down and drew his rifle.

The gunfire stopped abruptly. Slocum came to the lip of a dish-shaped hollow in the grassland. A small pond at the bottom afforded some water for a herd—or flock. A few sheep lay beside the pond, leaking blood into the water.

A steady string of what had to be curses echoed across the hollow. Slocum didn't understand a single word and knew this had to be the Basque sheepherder. The invective was met by more gunfire, both rifle and pistol.

Slocum got a better idea of where the gunfight was getting more deadly by the minute and turned his horse in that direction. He saw a man in a sheepskin hat occasionally pop up from behind a rock and fire a rifle that ended in a bell-shaped muzzle. Slocum knew from a single discharge that this was the weapon whose report he could not identify. Turning in the saddle, he followed the line of fire to a tumble of rocks where two men fired steadily.

Slocum began firing at the men behind the rocks and shouted to the sheepherder to let him ride up.

Slocum didn't understand the man's challenge, so he answered in Spanish, hoping this would be understood. All it did was make the man turn his blunderbuss on Slocum.

"I'm trying to help you, dammit!" Slocum hit the ground and let his mare run off. He staggered a few steps and fell facedown. He began squeezing off one round after another to keep Blevins and Cooper under cover.

As he fired, a thought came to Slocum that made him more furious than ever. Caleb Tewksbury had abandoned the Basque to race to the ranch house when he should have stayed and fought. It was as much as he expected from any of the Tewksbury clan. They never seemed to do anything, but were always the victims.

Slocum got a clear view of the gunman using the six-shooter.

"Cooper!" Slocum reared up and snapped a quick shot at the man but was in too big a hurry. His shot went wild, but his shout caused the murderous gunman to stand and peer across the meadow.

"Who's that?" Cooper shouted. "Who are you?"

"You shot Hez Clayton in the back," Slocum answered. "You remember him?"

"Who are you?"

Slocum ignored the six-shooter slugs whining around, all fired by the man he took to be Matt Blevins. He stood and walked forward, rifle in his left hand and his right itching to go for his Colt.

"Let's settle this right now, Cooper."

"Slocum!"

The gunman lifted his pistol and started firing as wildly as Slocum had with his rifle. A cold calm settled on Slocum as his hand circled the butt of his six-shooter, drew and fired. His aim was good, but the distance was extreme. Cooper grunted, staggered back a step and reached for his belly. Slocum's bullet had struck the large belt buckle, and distance had robbed it of any carrying power. Slocum fired again, but Cooper was already taking cover.

"Come on, Cooper, die like a man. But that's asking too much of a snake like you, isn't it? You've never shot anyone facing you, have you? You shoot them in the back, like you did Clayton!"

Slocum started walking toward the rocks, the bullets whistling through the air, getting closer and closer. He ignored them and focused only on plugging Andy Cooper.

"Get away. Ride, dammit, let's get outta here!" Cooper cried. Slocum kept walking and firing. By the time he reached the rocks, all he found was spent brass and tracks leading away. He shoved his six-gun into its holster and scrambled to the top of the rocks, hoping for one last brief glimpse of the two men. This time he wouldn't rush his shot from the rifle.

To Slocum's disgust, they were gone. He slid down and

walked back toward the Basque sheepherder, his hands up in the air.

"Don't shoot that old gun at me," he called.

When he reached the spot where the Basque had been, he found only crushed grass and a small keg of black powder the man had used to load his blunderbuss. Slocum had seen similar weapons before and decided the shepherd had no idea what kind of gun to carry. The blunderbuss was more like a carbine in size but with an even shorter range. Its shot pattern was smaller than that from a real shotgun.

He heard an impressive string of curses coming from the direction of the pond and went to see if the Basque was injured. The man had dropped his old weapon and was on his knees beside a dead sheep. He held it in his arms as if it was a recently deceased member of his family.

Hot dark eyes fixed on Slocum as a torrential outpouring of incomprehensible guttural words left the man's lips. Then he switched to broken English Slocum could hardly understand.

"Sheep they kill. Awful men! Kill my sheep!"

"They wanted to kill you," Slocum pointed out.

"Ten—more!" The Basque got to his feet and started pointing to each dead sheep. "More, more! They kill for no reason."

"They have good reason," Slocum said. "They're cattlemen and you're a sheepherder. Worse, they have a grudge against your boss." Slocum looked up as Tewksbury and Caleb finally rode up. He wondered if they had hung back long enough to be certain the fight was finished.

"Damn, they're killin' my sheep," Tewksbury exclaimed.

"They're not yours. You're only letting them graze here. They belong to the Daggs brothers."

"If I got 'em on my land, they're mine!" Tewksbury said. "That was Old Man Blevins, wasn't it?"

"I don't know him, but the son of a bitch with him was certainly Andy Cooper."

"His back-shooter of a son," Caleb said. Both Slocum and Tewksbury ignored him.

"I want to go after him, and I want you two to come with me," Slocum said. "This is as much your fight as mine."

"More, Slocum, it's a damn sight more!" Tewksbury prodded one of the dead sheep with the toe of his boot, much to the sheepherder's consternation. "I got to pay the Daggs boys fer ever' one of the sheep what's killed."

"Twenny, they kill twenny," the Basque said.

"That's gonna cost me a small fortune if they keep it up. Caleb, you up for some killin'?"

"Sure thing, Pa," he said, but he didn't sound too enthusiastic about it.

"I go with you," the sheepherder said. "My friends . . ." He pointed to each of the sheep shot down by Blevins and Cooper.

"Stay here," Slocum said. "Watch over the rest of the flock. The Tewksburys and I'll stop the slaughter."

"Make food for you," the Basque said, his eyes fixed on a large sheep.

"Do that. We'll be back before you know it," Slocum said.

"I . . . I can stay with him and make sure nuthin' happens," Caleb suggested.

"Do whatever you want," Slocum said. He had no time for cowards. He found his mare and mounted, getting his bearings. Blevins and Cooper had ridden straight north toward the boundary of the Blevins spread. To the east was Graham's ranch land and west and south was all Circle T property.

"You ready?" Slocum asked as he reloaded his six-shooter. He checked his saddlebags and saw he had a spare cylinder with all six chambers charged and ready to pop into his pistol to save time reloading.

"We're ready," Tewksbury said. He nudged his son, who reluctantly mounted. Slocum wondered if they would be any help at all when he ran Cooper to ground. All he could hope for was that Caleb didn't shoot him in the back by accident.

He set out on the trail, with Tewksbury and Caleb struggling to match the pace he set. But as hard as he rode, he not only failed to overtake the two sheep killers, but lost their trail entirely not two miles from the pond.

"It looks like they turned to smoke," Caleb said. "We better git on back."

"Blevins's spread is ahead?"

"Five miles more," Tewksbury said. "It'll be past dark when you git there, Slocum. Cooper's not gonna ride away, not while his pa needs him."

"Not while there's a back waiting to be shot at," Slocum said angrily. He knew Tewksbury was right. There would be another day for another fight. Continuing into the heart of the enemy ranch was foolish since Blevins and Cooper had plenty of time to arrange an ambush. Without knowing how many gunmen he faced, Slocum was willing to concede the point to Tewksbury.

"We can try some of that mutton," Caleb said. "I don't know about you two, but my backbone's rubbin' against my belly."

"Fancy that," Slocum said. "You actually have a backbone?"

"Slocum," Tewksbury said sharply, "there's no call insultin' my boy."

Slocum ignored the rancher and headed back to the pond, but as he drew closer uneasiness turned to caution.

"What's the matter, Slocum?" asked Tewksbury when he saw how Slocum slowed to a walk.

"Something's wrong."

"What?" Caleb was anxious again. "I don't see nuthin' wrong."

"Take a deep breath. What do you smell?"

"Well, nuthin'," Caleb said.

"That's the problem. The Basque said he was going to cook up some sheep meat. I don't even smell a fire, much less roasting mutton."

"Might be he's takin' longer'n we thought to slaughter one of the woollies. Did you see the way he treated 'em? Like they was kin," said Tewksbury.

Slocum rode faster through the gathering gloom and reached the pond ahead of the Tewksburys. He dropped down and walked to where a body was stretched out on the ground. The Basque's sightless eyes watched nothing at all. Slocum closed the man's eyes and looked him over. The sheepherder was dressed in wool clothing, hot for Arizona but probably all he had to wear.

The clothing would be his shroud.

"What happened?" Tewksbury finally reached a spot where he could look down from horseback.

Slocum rolled the sheepherder over to expose the bullet hole in the middle of his back.

"Andy Cooper came back," Slocum said. "He might as well have left a signed confession."

In the distance sheep bleated and then fell silent as they returned to their grazing. The Basque had had no more chance against a man like Cooper than did the sheep when it came time for the slaughter.

11

Cooper would show up eventually. Slocum was sure of it as he paced back and forth like a caged animal. He had left his horse out of sight in a small forested area while he stalked a hill from one side to the other alert for any trace of dust showing riders coming this way. Slocum stopped his pacing and stared down the hill at the watering hole where dozens of sheep drank. Not twenty feet away was a small grave, a simple one with a crude wood above it where Slocum had buried the sheepherder. There should have been more, but there ought to be more for any decent, law-abiding man.

Any man other than Andy Cooper—Andy Blevins. Him Slocum would gladly leave out in the hot Arizona sun for the buzzards and hope they wouldn't choke on Cooper's vile flesh.

The sheep scattered around the pasture hardly kept Slocum occupied, as a herd of cattle would. There was something dull about the docile creatures where a cow was more active and had more character. Slocum knew neither animal was too bright, but he dealt with cattle better than sheep. How the Basque sheepherder had learned to love the woolly animals was beyond Slocum, as was a fate that brought the man from the northern part of Spain across an ocean and a continent to be murdered by a bullet in the back.

Slocum kept looking northward toward the Blevins spread—or where Tewksbury said it started. There weren't fences in that part of the Tonto Basin, and Slocum suspected any man could claim grazing rights. Since the sheepherder had been so brutally murdered, Tewksbury had been gone from his ranch. Lydia had been evasive about her father's whereabouts, but Caleb had let it slip that John Tewksbury was rounding up allies for the fight with Blevins. The feud hadn't ended with Graham's murder.

"Who killed that son of a bitch?" Slocum wondered aloud. About anyone could have since most had a motive. Slocum knew whoever had shot Graham had been trusted by the man. Either that or the killer had been good at sneaking up to catch him in his own parlor room without a six-shooter at hand. Slocum found it hard to believe Tewksbury had the skill or patience or courage to simply walk into that den of murderous thieves, shoot Graham and then leave. If Tewksbury had been responsible, he would have burned the house down or taken the stolen horses back. Slocum had found them in the corral.

"Lydia and Graham," he said, shaking his head. That was almost more than he could understand unless she wanted to get back at her pa. With the Tewksbury family anything was possible.

Slocum stopped his restless patrol and stared across the pasture to the east. A tiny speck moved faster than a cow might. He picked up his field glasses and watched almost a minute before he made out the solitary rider coming his way. Slocum checked his rifle to be sure it had a full magazine, then sank to the ground in a prone position and sighted in on the rider.

A a sudden glint stopped Slocum from squeezing off a shot. He grabbed his field glasses and studied the rider more carefully. When he made out the lawman's badge on the rider's vest, Slocum cursed. He wanted to handle Cooper in his own way, without a sheriff butting in.

He put his field glasses away and rested the rifle against a rock where he could grab it fast, if the man proved to be an impostor. But as he made his way up the hill, muttering under his breath, Slocum got a better look at him. After a lot of years, Slocum could spot a lawman immediately. Something about the way he carried himself, or the tacit assumption everyone would obey if he gave a command, or maybe just outright arrogance. Slocum had seen cowardly marshals and brave ones, and they were all cut from the same cloth.

"Howdy," Slocum called.

"You must be Slocum," the lawman said. He wiped sweat off his face and dismounted.

"How do you come by that?" Slocum asked.

"Been over at the Tewksbury house," the lawman said. "I'm deputy sheriff over in Prescott. Name's Drury, Slick Drury." The lawman cocked his head to one side, squinted a little and studied Slocum closely. "You heard of me?"

"Can't say that I have."

"Well, mister, Deputy Sheriff Drury don't take kindly to bein' lied to."

"Then you'll find yourself in a world of misery around here," Slocum said. He edged toward his rifle when the deputy reached for the six-shooter hanging at his side.

"Don't go mouthin' off to me," Drury said, color coming to his already florid face until he looked like a stewed tomato. "I hate it and have cut down men because they didn't know when to stay quiet."

Slocum said nothing.

"So?"

"What do you want, Deputy?"

"I can see I'm gonna have trouble with you." Drury looked around at the sheep. "These your woollies?"

"No."

"You don't say much, do you? What's your name?"

"Slocum, and you made it real clear you don't cotton to anyone running off at the mouth."

"I got a murder to look into."

"The sheepherder's grave is down there by the pond," Slocum said.

"What? I don't know nuthin' about any sheepherder. I'm here to find who killed Tom Graham."

Slocum studied the deputy and sized him up as a blowhard probably being paid by someone in the Blevins camp to kick up dust around Tewksbury and his family. From all Slocum had seen, this wouldn't be too hard, but the deputy had to overlook a powerful lot—like Blevins's son, Andy Cooper.

"What do you know about Graham getting himself killed?" Drury was getting mad.

"That's about it. Graham's dead. You don't care that a Basque was shot in the back?"

"I don't know anything about that," Drury said. "Might be I ought to run you in. What'd you say your name was?"

"Slocum." This caused Slocum to fall into a deadly calm. If the deputy meant it, even an incompetent lawman could find a wanted poster or two with Slocum's likeness.

"Let's start over, Slocum. I'm Deputy Sheriff Drury and I'm here to find who murdered Tom Graham. Mr. Graham was a decent, law-abiding man, and not finding his murderer would be a terrible blot on my escutcheon. And my escutcheon's damn good runnin' down killers."

"I don't know who killed him," Slocum said.

"But you got an opinion on who might have. What is it?"

"From what I hear, Graham wasn't the most likable cuss. Might have been a lot of people."

"I'm thinkin' it was John Tewksbury. You work for him, don't you?"

"Can't say that's exactly right," Slocum said. "He owes me money for work I did breaking mustangs. I'm watching his sheep after the sheepherder was shot in the back." Slocum saw no interest flare in the deputy's eyes at the mention again of the Basque's murder.

"You might have plugged Graham for him. You have the look of being mighty familiar with that six-gun of yours."

Slocum considered what to do, since Drury already had his mind made up about Graham's death and was only looking for someone in Tewksbury's camp to pin it on.

"You ever hear of Andy Cooper?"

"That's one of Blevins's boys, isn't it?"

"His son. Cooper changed his name after a shoot-out down Texas way."

"Not my worry. I've got a murderer running around the Basin needin' to be brought to justice. Why don't you ride with me, Slocum?"

"You arresting me?"

"Nope, not yet. But you're mighty high on my list of possible murderers." Drury stared hard at Slocum, then glanced away. "It's to your benefit to help me find who done shot Graham."

"Otherwise, you'll figure I did it and arrest me?" Slocum asked.

The deputy shrugged and looked back. He couldn't match Slocum's cold stare.

"You cooperatin' or you need some persuadin'?"

"Looking after a pasture full of sheep's not my idea of a way to spend the day," Slocum said. "Where are you going to start looking for Graham's killer?"

"Need to talk to Matt Blevins. His spread's not far from here. Saddle up and let's ride."

Slocum almost balked at the deputy's assumption he would go along with him, but then he relented. Looking after Tewksbury's sheep wasn't a fit job for anyone, unless you were a Basque sheepherder by birth. More than this, Slocum wasn't likely to do anything to find Andy Cooper waiting for him to come kill more sheep. Better to ride into the Blevins ranch with a lawman beside him, even if the deputy had already convicted Tewksbury of the crime.

Slocum reached for his rifle but saw the deputy whip out his six-shooter.

"You want me to leave my rifle here?" Slocum asked the deputy.

"Reckon not. Be careful how you swing that around," the deputy warned.

Slocum got his mare and joined the impatient deputy.

"You been a deputy long?" Slocum asked.

"Why're you askin'?"

"You seem to know the folks in these parts pretty well," Slocum said. "How long did you work for Matt Blevins?"

"Six months," Drury said before he realized he was telling Slocum things that he shouldn't. "I only worked as a hand, chasing strays."

"That seems to be mostly what cowboys do in the Basin," Slocum said. He wondered how many of Tewksbury's cattle Drury had rustled while working for Blevins. Even if he had been pure as the wind-driven snow, Drury had to be beholden to his former employer. Slocum began to wonder how smart it was riding anywhere with Drury.

"I got hired as deputy over in Prescott a couple months back, and I take my job seriously." Drury pursed his lips, then glanced at Slocum. "Who found Graham's body?"

"Never heard who reported it to the law," Slocum said carefully. For all he knew, he wasn't the first one to come across Graham's body. But if he had contacted the sheriff's office, he would have been thrown in jail so fast his head would have spun until they dropped the noose around his neck.

"You know a gent named Murphy?"

"He was Graham's foreman," Slocum said. "Him and me locked horns early on."

"Do tell."

"He and two others tried to ambush me when I stopped them from rustling Tewksbury's cattle."

"Hadn't heard that part of it," Drury said. He sucked on his gums awhile longer. "That makes sense from what I know of Murphy. He's had quite a history of liberatin' other people's cattle."

"Liberating?" Slocum laughed harshly. "That's a mighty fancy word for stealing."

"Murphy said he thought maybe you had killed his boss. Said you were stealing horses when Graham caught you, and you murdered him."

"What horses are these? Check Tewksbury's corral. All have his Circle T brand—and it's easy enough to see if someone's run the brand. I don't even know what Graham's brand was. All the cows I ever saw on his spread were stolen."

"Graham used the Double Bar G. You're right. That's hard to change into Circle T, but one thing I've found, where there's a cow or horse to be stolen, there's determination on the part of the thief."

Slocum mulled over what the deputy had said. Murphy might have killed his employer, but the motive was unguessable. Had Murphy seen Slocum taking the horses that had been stolen earlier or was the man guessing? He might be doing nothing but accusing wildly because he had nothing to lose placing blame on Slocum and ultimately John Tewksbury. Somehow, Slocum thought Murphy had seen him taking the horses and fixed him for killing Graham.

"What about Murphy's story don't you believe?"

"Everything. He couldn't look me in the eye when he was tellin' his story. Sounded like something he had been schooled to say, too. Got real confused when I asked questions."

Slocum saw the main gate leading to the Blevins spread ahead. He slid the leather thong off the hammer of his Colt, just to be ready should the lead start flying.

"Don't go touchin' that pistol of yours again," Drury warned. "And stay in front of me where I can watch you."

"I won't let any of Blevins's men throw down on me," Slocum warned.

"I won't let 'em," Drury said sharply. "I'm a deputy sheriff."

Slocum didn't have that much confidence in Drury awing Blevins—or Andy Cooper.

"You check wanted posters at your office before you came here?"

"No need. The only crime I'm interested in is Tom Graham's murder." Drury pulled hard on his reins, stopped a dozen yards from the front door of Blevins's house and waited for Old Man Blevins and three of his cowboys to come out. Slocum pulled down the brim of his hat to block the sun so he could get a better look at the men. None was Andy Cooper.

"Afternoon, Mr. Blevins," Drury said loudly. "You got a minute or two so we can talk?"

"I know you," Blevins said, stepping out so his men could spread to either side of him. All of them looked nervous, hands twitching and fingers tapping nervously against their holsters. If one of them got spooked and started throwing lead, there wasn't a chance in hell of Drury and Slocum escaping. Even Matt Blevins looked uneasy that the deputy had shown up on his doorstep.

"Used to work for Tom Graham," Drury said. "That's why the sheriff sent me. I'm familiar with the people and the lay of the Basin."

"Don't know nothin' 'bout Tom's death. Don't know anything other than I'm not going to let it go unpunished."

"No good takin' the law into your own hands, Mr. Blevins," Drury said. "I'm here to make it all legal."

"Then why isn't he in shackles? And why's he still got his gun?" Blevins pointed straight at Slocum.

"He's lendin' a hand as I poke around. You know anything about the circumstances surroundin' the killing?"

"I heard that this one was stealin' horses. Might be Graham caught him, and he gunned him down."

"Your son around? I'd like to talk to Andy."

"Why? He don't know about this. He wasn't even back from Texas yet when Graham was shot."

"I thought he might have somethin' to say. Him and Tom had words before he left for Texas, if I remember rightly."

"You don't. My son's never had a quarrel with Graham."

"Why don't I ask him myself? Is Andy here?" Drury looked around, as if he might peer through solid walls.

"I told you he wasn't here. Don't know where he is or when he'll be back. Might not be back."

"That'd be a shame. Makes him look . . . guilty," Drury said.

Slocum tensed when Blevins reached for the hogleg on his hip and the three men with him started for their six-shooters, too.

"You git off my property. And take that murderer with you."

"I'd hoped for a little more cooperation," Drury said. "I need to ask some questions over at the Circle T and then I might be back to see if Andy's shown up."

"Do that," Blevins said. "Just ride on out of here now. If you don't, I might decide Slocum's lookin' too guilty to let go."

"Good afternoon, Mr. Blevins," Drury said, nodding in the rancher's direction. He jerked his head, indicating Slocum ought to precede him from the yard. As he rode, Slocum felt an itch run from his belt all the way up his spine to his neck and then head back down as he waited for a bullet to kill him. Andy Cooper's specialty was back-shooting, and Slocum was sure the man was hiding out around the ranch.

"That didn't go as good as I'd hoped," Drury said. "I need to talk to Andy, but with you along there's not much chance of that. You and him have a quarrel?"

"He shot my partner in the back down in San Antonio," Slocum said straight out. "I've never known him to face anyone when he gunned them down."

"So you figure he's responsible for killing that sheep-herder of yours?"

"The Basque worked for Tewksbury or maybe he worked for the Daggs brothers up in Flagstaff. He wasn't 'my' sheepherder."

"You brought his killing up mighty fast, like it mattered to you."

"You're the lawman. Shouldn't anyone's murder matter to you?"

"I need to take care of one killing at a time. No reason to get all confused."

"You know Andy Cooper is responsible, don't you?"

"You're talkin' too much, Slocum. I don't much like that. When we get to the Circle T, you keep your tater trap shut. Understand?"

Slocum nodded. They got back on the road that wound around and eventually passed the Graham spread. Slocum looked up the road to the house, wondering if Blevins had been telling the truth about Cooper not even being in the Tonto Basin when Graham was killed. Probably not. But if he had to pin the crime on anyone, it'd be Murphy. Slocum had no idea what the foreman's reason for shooting his employer might be, but he had not been around the ranch house when Slocum came after the horses.

"If we cut across here, we can get to Tewksbury's faster," Drury said. He waited for Slocum to precede him and rode a few feet behind so he could cover Slocum.

They rode in silence for a spell, then Slocum tugged back on the reins and stood in the stirrups.

"What's wrong, Slocum? Why'd you stop?"

Slocum knew the deputy had drawn his six-gun, but that might be needed.

"Something's wrong. I can feel it. If—" Slocum never finished his sentence. A shot echoed across the meadow, followed quickly by the deputy's horse neighing and then galloping past. The lawman clung to the pommel but wobbled as he rode. Slocum saw that he had dropped his six-shooter—and he also saw the bright red spot spreading on Drury's back.

"Cooper!" Slocum roared as he wheeled his horse around. His Colt slid free of its holster as he hunted for a target. Wherever Cooper had fired from, he was gone now. "Cooper!"

Slocum's rage knew no bounds, but he couldn't go after

Cooper or whoever had ambushed them. The deputy was making funny noises as he flopped about, struggling to stay in the saddle. Slocum jammed his pistol back with savage fury and galloped after the deputy.

12

Slocum knew he had exhausted the horse when it began to falter as he galloped after the deputy. Hating it but seeing no alternative, he slowed and let the lawman disappear ahead behind a line of gently rising hills. If he hadn't eased back, his mare would have died under him. He let his horse slow to a walk for a few hundred yards, then trotted and finally worked his way through the hillocks and down into a grassy stretch. Finding the deputy wasn't hard. The man had fallen off his horse, which had run off once it was free of its rider.

Hitting the ground, Slocum ran to the fallen lawman and knelt. He raised Drury's head. From the man's condition, he was surprised when Drury's eyelids flickered and he stared up at Slocum.

"Hurts real bad inside," he said. "Can't hardly breathe without it hurtin' more. Help me."

"I'll get you to Tewksbury's," he said, "but your horse is gone. I'll have to let you ride mine, but she's all tuckered out. You ride, I'll walk. Can you hang on?"

"Got to. Can't let no back-shooter do me in. I'm Slick Drury, meanest, baddest lawman this side of the Rio Grande." Drury tried to smile and ended up coughing. Slocum said nothing when he saw the pink froth on the

117

deputy's lips. The bullet had gone clean through one of his lungs. If he wasn't taken care of fast, he wouldn't last more than a few minutes.

"You a chewin' man?" Slocum asked.

"Got some chaw in my vest pocket. Take some. I . . . I can't." Drury coughed up more blood.

Slocum searched the deputy and found the chewing tobacco. He stripped open the foil and threw away the tobacco, then he used his knife to cut away the man's bloodied shirt. Not much blood leaked out, either where the bullet had entered or where it had exited his chest, but Slocum saw the ragged flesh rippling as the air went into the holes and came out the man's mouth. Slocum tore the foil in half, pressed one piece against the hole in Drury's back and repeated the process in the front before using strips of shirt to tie the foil into place.

"Doesn't hurt as much. What'd you do?"

"Don't talk." Slocum heaved Drury to his feet. The man took a surprisingly strong step and then collapsed. Carrying him, Slocum got the deputy up into the saddle. Drury started to topple, but Slocum grabbed him and held him upright. Before starting the long walk back to the Circle T, Slocum made sure the foil was secured over the two bullet holes. He looked around to be sure Cooper wasn't lying in wait, then took the mare's reins and started for Tewksbury's ranch house.

An hour later, Slocum spotted Caleb Tewksbury on the roof of the house. Like a prairie dog, he popped up and pointed, then slid down to the porch before yelling at the top of his lungs. Tewksbury and three of his cowboys had rushed out by the time Slocum reached the yard.

"What you got there, Slocum?" Tewksbury asked.

"He's a deputy from over in Prescott. We went to palaver with Blevins but didn't get too far. On the way back here someone back-shot him."

"Blevins?"

"Could have been, but it was probably Cooper," Slocum said. "That's the way he likes it."

"You didn't see who done the dirty deed?"

"Get him inside where we can tend him," Slocum said, letting Drury slip from the saddle. He caught the man's dead weight and stumbled back. Nobody moved to help him. "What's wrong with you? Help him!"

"Slocum, he's beyond help in this world."

Slocum lowered Drury to the ground and pressed his finger into the man's throat, looking for the pulse. Nothing. He put his finger under the deputy's nose to test for hot air coming out. Nothing. He looked up at Tewksbury, anger mixing with his helplessness. The rancher had seen what he hadn't—what he hadn't wanted to admit. Slick Drury was deader than a doornail and might have been for most of the ride back to the ranch.

"There's going to be hell explaining this," Slocum said. "A deputy sheriff getting shot in the back means every last one of the sheriff's men will be here in a flash."

"Might be," Tewksbury said thoughtfully. "Might not. The sheriff's not what you'd call an ambitious galoot. Most likely, he'll think on the matter fer a week or two after we let him know what's happened."

"You're not going to tell the sheriff his deputy's dead, are you?"

"What's in it fer us if I do?"

"You need all the help you can get to fight Blevins and Cooper," Slocum said. "The law's not too inclined to take your side right now. If you try to hide the deputy's murder, it'll make it seem you had a hand in it."

"I've been workin' on this in my own way," Tewksbury said.

"What have you done?"

"Been out talkin' to other ranchers here in the Basin. Got a fair number of 'em agreein' with me 'bout Blevins. Graham was better liked, though I don't see why. But Blevins has ruffled feathers fer years."

"You told them about Cooper being back?"

"Most don't remember Blevins's boy when he was here before," Tewksbury said. "Those that do ain't happy

Andy's home, no, sirree. He was the kind of little bastard that'd shoot yer favorite dog just to watch it die."

"How'd you get anyone to join up with you after you brought in the sheep to graze?"

"Kinda forgot to tell 'em 'bout that," Tewksbury admitted. "Jist kept hammerin' away that Blevins was gonna do what he done to Graham and steal ever'one's land."

"You think Blevins killed Graham?"

"Him or Andy. Prob'ly Andy, since Old Man don't git his hands dirty if he kin avoid it."

Slocum tried to make sense of it. He doubted Tewksbury had murdered Graham, but that didn't mean Caleb or one of the others in a circle about him right now hadn't pulled the trigger. Or Murphy. He knew the foreman was a sniveling son of a bitch. Slocum sagged. Tewksbury might even be right that Blevins or Cooper had pulled the trigger. The only thing against Andy Cooper being responsible for the murder was that Graham had been shot in the face. Even unarmed, Graham would have intimidated a coward like Cooper.

"You got a cemetery around here where we can bury him?" Slocum stood and backed away from the deputy. He hadn't much liked Drury but wanted to do right by him.

"We kin plant him out where you buried the Basque. They might enjoy each other's company."

Slocum wondered what he was going to do. Graham's death was one thing, but a deputy being shot in the back wasn't going to set well with anyone over in the territorial capital.

"I can read you like a book, Slocum," said Tewksbury. "You're thinkin' on moseyin' on, ain't ya?"

"The thought crossed my mind." Slocum considered the horses he had been promised and the cattle and decided it was better to get away with his hide intact than to make a few dollars selling the animals.

"He won't let ya."

"Blevins?"

"Cooper. I see it in yer eyes. I bet it's in his, too. There's no way two of you'll be alive much longer. One of you's got to take out the other. That's the way it is," Tewksbury said.

For all the man's crooked ways, he saw right into a man's soul. Slocum had to laugh ruefully. Maybe that was what made Tewksbury as successful a crook as he was, if anything he had done so far in the Tonto Basin could be called successful. The laugh died when Slocum realized how Tewksbury had hit him smack dab in the one spot he couldn't justify away. If for nothing else, he owed his dead partner a touch of justice.

Six-gun justice.

"There's no point pussyfooting around any longer," Slocum said, coming to a decision. "You get the deputy buried, and I'll take care of Cooper."

"You want to do it all by yer lonesome? Me and the rest of the boys kin back your play. By tomorrow noon I'll have a couple dozen others here. Like I said, I been askin' 'round and got quite a posse lined up to take care of them sidewinders over at Blevins's place."

"I don't need an army. All I need is hanging on my hip." He touched the ebony handle of his six-gun as much to re-assure himself as to show Tewksbury what he intended.

"You're a damn fool if you don't wait fer the rest to git here," Tewksbury said. "Cooper's sneaky. He done proved that a couple times with bullets to men's backs." He tapped the deputy's body with the toe of his boot. "We'll need all the firepower we can muster, but the rest of the ranchers won't be here till tomorrow morning."

"I need to rest up a mite," Slocum said, "get some supplies and more ammo. Have the stableboy tend my horse, too."

"Good," Tewksbury said. "You might want to talk with Lydia. She's been askin' 'bout you ever since you went out to watch over the flock fer me."

"She in the house?"

"Ain't seen her lately, but I reckon so. Now, you get some grub and rest up. We got a big fight on our hands," Tewksbury said. He waved to his men and they went to the barn for a big powwow. Slocum wondered what plans Tewksbury had in mind but wasn't willing to sit through the man's long-winded recitation to find out. He wiped his hands on his jeans and went to the front door. He started to knock, then decided there was no point. Lydia was the only one inside, and she was the one he wanted to have a few words with.

Slocum went in and called, "Lydia? Where are you?" Not finding her, he quickly searched the house. Her bedroom was small, neat and somehow at odds with the way he thought of her—wild and wanton. Everything in the room was precisely placed, not a speck of dust showed anywhere, the armoire was polished and the linens clean.

He went back onto the porch and looked around. Slocum frowned when he started toward the barn and got a look at the corral behind it. Star wasn't in the corral. His stride lengthened, and he jumped up onto the lower rail in the corral fence. His quick eyes worked over each and every horse in the pen, and Star was not there or in the other, smaller corral some distance away.

He went into the barn, where Tewksbury had his men sitting on hay bales and was lecturing them. Tewksbury stopped and looked at Slocum when he came barging in.

"What's wrong, Slocum?"

"You said Lydia was in the house. Her horse isn't in the corral. Where'd she go?"

"Danged if I know. Last I saw her she *was* in the house. Caleb, you know where your sister's off to?"

Caleb shrugged and looked down at the barn floor as if finding some revelation there. The rest of the men shook their heads and looked puzzled.

"Caleb," Slocum said sharply. "Where's Lydia?"

"Well, she was talkin' 'bout goin' out to see you. Least I think that was what she said. I wasn't payin' a whole lot of attention. Pa had me up on the roof as lookout."

"She left? She left without tellin' me?" Tewksbury roared and launched a punch that knocked Caleb ass over teakettle. "You idiot! You blithering fool! Blevins wants the whole damned lot of us dead! What'd he do if he got Lydia?"

"Kill her?" Caleb's voice came out as a squeak.

"Of course he would, you fool!"

Slocum left Tewksbury to berating his son and slipped out of the barn. He mounted and rode to the small corral where Lydia had kept Star. The dirt around the corral was cut up from too many horses passing by. He began a wider arc and thought he found tracks leading to the north. It didn't much matter if this was Lydia's track or not. He had toyed with Tewksbury's notion of letting him and his men back him up when he rode to Blevins's ranch, but after seeing how Tewksbury and his son acted, Slocum thought he was better off riding alone.

The hoofprints became clearer as he got away from the barn and the house. He rode faster, hoping to overtake the rider and identify who rode ahead. When he reached a hillock looking down into the vast pastureland where the sheep contentedly grazed, he saw Lydia ahead. Those had been her tracks.

"Lydia!" No response. He shouted a second time and this time got her attention. She turned and looked around. He thought she saw him, but she didn't acknowledge him before she rode on. Slocum swore under his breath. She was heading straight for Blevins's spread.

He pushed his tired horse as hard as he could and narrowed the distance between them, but his mare had been ridden too hard all day long and began to falter. Slocum started to call to Lydia again and then bit back her name. Three riders angled into the rangeland, laughing and joshing one another. A bottle passed between them. Slocum led his horse to a ravine and then tethered the horse. It would be a while before the overheated horse regained enough energy to carry him after Lydia. Until then, Slocum wanted to stay both hidden and alive.

"Where'd he get off to?" one rider asked loudly.

"What's the dif'rence? He kin take care of hisse'f."

"Let's go shoot some of them sheep. I wanna see if I kin stampede 'em."

"You can't. They're too dumb to run."

Slocum's hand flew to his six-gun when a shot rang out. A loud bleat was followed by the sound of a heavy body falling to the ground. Slocum scrambled up the side of the ravine and peered over the rim. The three drunk riders had their six-shooters out and were taking aim at a few sheep that had wandered over.

"Wanna see if I kin shoot one with my eyes closed." The cowboy began firing. Slocum ducked as a bullet whined past his head. The man would have spotted him if he'd had his eyes open.

"Got another one," a cowboy said, laughing at his drunken marksmanship.

"You shot my ma," Slocum called out in a high-pitched voice. "Stop killing my family or I'll get you."

"What's that?" All three men looked around. "You hear that?"

"Musta been the wind."

"You're murdering my family," Slocum called out. "Stop killing us."

He poked his head up enough to see the three drunks looking at one another, eyes wide. They stared at the pistols in their hands and then at the sheep they had shot. With a yelp, they put their spurs to their horses and rocketed away. Slocum kept from laughing too hard and then sobered. Tewksbury had a hard row to hoe grazing the sheep in the Tonto Basin. Most all of the ranchers weren't inclined to think too highly of the animals.

Slocum knew he had been lucky that these three had been drinking so heavily in the middle of the day and hadn't expected anyone else to be on the range. He slid down the slope and sat as he thought hard what to do. Getting rid of the three was easy compared with catching up with Lydia. He had no idea why she was heading to Matt Blevins's ranch, but like the rest of her family, she didn't often show too much good sense.

He wouldn't put it past her to think she could talk Blevins out of his range war.

"You rested up?" Slocum asked his horse. The mare shook her head as if denying she was ready to ride ahead. He didn't blame her. He was tired, too, but Lydia needed to have some sense pounded into her hard head. Slocum patted the mare's neck and wished he had a lump of sugar for her, but he didn't. His own belly growled so hard from lack of food he wished he had stayed at the Tewksbury ranch for one more meal. Then he remembered how Tewksbury was getting his allies ready for a major bloodbath in the Basin and knew he couldn't be caught between the two feuding factions.

"Settle up with Cooper and then I'm out of here," he said. "Even working for the Daggs brothers up in Flagstaff seems like a better life right now."

He kept talking to the mare to reassure her as he walked her slowly from the ravine and looked around for the three drunk cowboys. They had disappeared like smoke in the wind. That made riding northward a little easier, but Slocum worried they might have gone to earth somewhere between here and the ranch. He had scared them for a spell, but they weren't likely to remember too long, depending on how much more tarantula juice they swilled and how much Dutch courage it gave them.

Slocum got his bearings and changed direction, going to the far side of the pastureland, cutting through a small wooded area and out onto a hill near the Blevins ranch. He started to shout again when he saw Lydia riding along a trail. Ahead to her right were the three drunk cowboys. Slocum judged distances and knew the trio was too far for him to shoot, even if he had a rifle with a longer barrel than that on the Winchester. Shouting at her would draw unwanted attention to both him and the woman who rode along oblivious to her danger.

Slocum started down the hillside, intent on diverting the three. Then he saw a new danger threatening Lydia. He grabbed for his rifle and pulled it to his shoulder. His horse shifted nervously under him so that accurately aiming was increasingly difficult.

"Cooper," he said with venom in the name. Slocum tried to settle the mare down but she refused.

Lydia didn't see Cooper coming up from her rear, and then it was impossible. Cooper was between him and Lydia. If he missed the murderous outlaw, he might hit Lydia.

Then Slocum thought that might be a boon for her. Cooper put on a spurt of speed at the last moment and caught up with her. As she turned and finally saw him, Cooper reached out and grabbed her, his hand clamping down hard on her mouth to cut off any outcry.

They struggled for a moment, then Lydia subsided.

Together they rode for the Blevins ranch.

13

Slocum sheathed his rifle and fumed at his bad luck—and Lydia's stupidity in coming so far into enemy country. He cut off the trail and swung wide, going away from the three drunk cowboys who sat in a row like crows on the fence and chattered on. He'd gotten some small pleasure out of scaring them the way he had, but the gloating went away fast when he realized they forced him to circle and gave Cooper time to take his prisoner to the ranch house.

As he rode, he wondered why Cooper had stopped Lydia from calling out. A man like him would enjoy a woman's screams of fear. She had also given in so easily that Slocum wondered what Cooper had said to her.

He emerged some distance from the Blevins house and studied the area around it, hoping to catch sight of Lydia and Cooper. The pair had disappeared, but the roundabout path he had taken to get to this point had given them plenty of time to be about anywhere on the ranch. The barn? He saw no trace of Star in the corral outside, but Cooper might have put the horse into the barn to keep any casual visitor from asking about it and its rider. Worse than the barn, Cooper might have taken her to his pa's house. It was larger than the Tewksbury residence and three times the size of Graham's house. Even if Slocum got inside without being seen, prowling about such a large building would be dangerous.

As dangerous to Lydia as it was to him.

Slocum went cold when he saw a half dozen riders come from the east. They dismounted and went into the house. Less than ten minutes later, four more showed up. All had the hard look of gunmen ready for a fight. Tewksbury had recruited other ranchers from around the Tonto Basin to his cause, but Blevins had gone outside the region and brought in killers.

There was a fight brewing, and it would be brutal. In spite of the hired guns already inside the Blevins house, Slocum started down the slope toward it. He had to get Lydia free before so many men arrived that it would take an army to pry her loose—if it could be done at all without killing her. Slocum never forgot that Cooper preferred to shoot men in the back. Murdering a woman would be even easier and more pleasurable for him.

He had gone only a part of the way down the gentle slope when the three drunks rode into the yard. They were still jumpy from the ghost of the sheep they had killed talking to them and had their hands on the butts of their six-shooters. Worse than this, they were more alert than the other gunmen had been, looking around nervously as if the sheep spirit had followed them and would turn them into a barbecue if they relaxed vigilance for even an instant.

Slocum veered off at an angle, not slowing or increasing his speed, to keep from drawing unwanted attention. One of the drunks spotted him and shouted something. Slocum kept his head down, to prevent his face from being seen, and waved, as if he belonged here and was too busy to ride over and be friendly.

His attitude kept the three from getting any more suspicious than they were. They put their heads together, one pointed again at Slocum, then the trio dismounted and went inside the house. Slocum heaved a deep sigh and kept riding, hitting the trail where Cooper had captured Lydia and riding back along it. He fought down a rising anger at

Cooper but knew there wasn't anything he could do about him and his back-shooting, kidnapping ways alone. He had thought he could fight Blevins and the rest of his rustlers by himself, but he had to admit Tewksbury was right. The more ranchers who banded together for this battle, the better.

"You ain't mistaken, Slocum? Ya know this fer a certain thing sure?" Tewksbury showed all the emotions Slocum had expected. Anger faded to concern for his daughter and then was replaced by an even bigger hatred. As the hatred burned itself out, concern came again and started the cycle anew.

"I saw it with my own eyes," Slocum said. "I tried to reach her when I spotted her, but Cooper got to her first. Why was she riding to the Blevins spread?"

Slocum looked around the tight circle of men intently listening to his story. Not a one of them showed any comprehension as to Lydia's reasons.

"She's a headstrong gal," Tewksbury said. "Might be she was thinkin' she could act as go-between and work things out. That's as stupid as anything Caleb here's ever done."

Slocum saw Caleb bristle at this but said nothing.

"Cooper hasn't sent a demand? Or Blevins?" Slocum wondered how long it would be until an unrealistic demand arrived. "Getting rid of the sheep in exchange for your daughter's life would be counting coup for them."

"He'd want me dead 'fore he wanted the sheep out of the Basin," Tewksbury said. "I'm goin' over and call him out. Hell, I'll take on both Blevins and his no-account son. I don't care! I want Lydia back!"

"I'll stand with you, Pa," Caleb said.

Tewksbury stared at his son for a moment, then nodded and slapped him on the back. "Good man. We're family. We Tewksburys got to stick together, no matter what they do to us."

"Two of you won't be enough." Slocum told of the gunmen he had seen going into the Tewksbury ranch house. "These were only the ones I spotted in a few minutes. Blevins might have fifty men scattered around his spread by now."

"They don't sound like folks from 'round here. Could be Cooper is callin' in his back-shootin' buddies from Texas and elsewhere," Tewksbury said, chewing on his lower lip as he thought hard on what Slocum revealed. "That means we got to go in, the lot of us, with guns blazin'. That's goin' to come to a sorry end if Lydia's caught in the middle."

"There's no other choice," Caleb said stoutly. "You said so yourself. We got to fight to get Lydia back. You want me to take a message to Blevins sayin' if anything happens to her, we'll bury the lot of 'em?"

"Threats won't work," Slocum said. "You're past that."

"All or nuthin', Slocum? That what you're sayin'?" Tewksbury fixed a gimlet eye on him.

"Every last rancher you can muster ought to go. A bluff won't win this pot."

"You got a scheme brewin' in that skull of yers?"

"I'll try to sneak in the back way when you and the rest of the ranchers draw Blevins's attention," Slocum said. "I have to find where Lydia is being kept, but that shouldn't be too hard." Slocum didn't want to say anything more, but Tewksbury forced him.

"How do you propose to do that, Slocum?"

"When you ride up, Cooper will join his pa and the rest of the gunmen. Wherever he comes from, that'll be where Lydia's being kept." Slocum hadn't wanted to be so blunt because it told Tewksbury that his daughter had already been violated by Andy Cooper.

"I'll kill him," Tewksbury said in an emotionless voice.

"Not if I get him in my sights first," Slocum said, "but rescuing Lydia is more important."

Tewksbury nodded once brusquely, then bellowed to his men to send the word to other ranchers about what would be required of them.

"And tell 'em to bring as many of their men as they kin," Tewksbury added. "If this is gonna be a fight, I want to be on the winnin' side."

Slocum had to agree.

More than forty men rode behind them as Slocum and Tewksbury turned from the road toward Blevins's house. It had taken a full day for the small army to assemble, but Slocum thought it was necessary. When he saw rifle barrels poking out from every window in the house and every knothole in the barn walls, he wondered if even forty was going to be enough.

"Hang back," Tewksbury ordered. "I'll ride ahead and palaver." He looked at Slocum and canted his head to one side. Slocum knew what they had planned, but sneaking around back didn't look as easy as he had hoped. There wasn't a chance to come up with a new plan, so Slocum fell back and let others surround him.

When enough of the angry, armed men had passed him, he handed his reins to Caleb and dropped to the ground, keeping low and trusting to his skills and Tewksbury's misdirection that none of Blevins's men saw him.

He skirted the broad yard to the east and flopped to his belly, wiggling closer to the house. He counted no fewer than three rifle barrels thrust from windows. Slocum stayed flat and watched, then smiled. The barrels didn't move an iota, telling him no gunman pulled the stocks to his shoulder or had a finger on the trigger. Blevins was only trying to puff himself up and make it appear he had more armed men on his side than he did.

Slocum got closer and then put his back to the wall of the house. A quick glance through the window startled both Slocum and the man inside the room. The rifle hadn't budged while Slocum approached, because the man sat back, feet up on the windowsill while he knocked back a shot or two from a whiskey bottle.

Grabbing fast, Slocum wrapped his fingers around the barrel and yanked to get it away from the inattentive sniper.

Slocum almost made it. The man yelped, dived and fired the rifle. The bullet went into the ground, but Slocum released the barrel as it heated from the bullet's passage. He went for his six-gun, but his fingers were clumsy from the burn. A second round had been fired past his head by the time Slocum shoved the muzzle of his Colt Navy through the window and fired point-blank into the sniper's belly.

Whatever discussion that might have been going on in front of the house ended in gunfire. Slocum fired at another man inside the house and missed. A hail of bullets forced him to duck out of the window and realize how dangerous his position was. He had meant to sneak into the house and prowl around until he found Lydia. Now that the men inside knew he was here, he had nowhere to hide, and if he ran, he would get shot in the back.

Slocum briefly thought the gunmen inside might fetch Cooper since back-shooting was the coward's speciality.

Then all he thought about was staying alive. Heavy footfalls inside warned him of someone coming. Slocum waited, then grabbed the rifle still poking out of the window and jerked down hard. When the stock met resistance, he popped up again and fired twice more. The gunman had been stunned by the stock catching him under the chin. Slocum's bullets ended his life.

Pulling the rifle out, Slocum reversed it and tried to fire into the house. This was dangerous because he had no idea where Lydia might be held, but there was no other chance for him to survive. He was forced down before he could squeeze off even a single shot. When the men inside the house started shooting through the wall, Slocum knew he had no choice but to retreat. Fast.

Running a zigzag pattern, he stayed clear of the wild shots following him to the drainage ditch he had crawled up to get this close to the house. Slocum dived and flopped hard into the ditch, then started crawling when tiny puffs of dust kicked up all around, as Blevins's men tried to ventilate him.

When he got back to the road, Slocum found a wild,

disorganized fight going on. The men with Tewksbury had taken shelter willy-nilly and their horses had run off, effectively pinning them where they lay.

Slocum saw Caleb some distance down the road and ran to him. The man stood with the reins of several horses clutched in his shaking hands. He was pale and his eyes were fixed on the road ahead.

"Snap out of it," Slocum said harshly. "Tether these horses, and go round up as many others as you can."

"I . . . I ought to be up there with Pa. He's bein' shot at."

"Get the horses. That's more important and will save more lives," Slocum said, searching through his saddlebags until he found his spare loaded cylinder. He knocked out the one with the six spent chambers and locked in the new cylinder. Then he found a box of shells and crammed them into his pocket. He wished he had brought more ammunition.

"I think he'd want me—"

"Do as I say. There's no way they can endure fire like that much longer," Slocum said. "We're going to ride out of here or be carried off to a cemetery. I'd rather ride, and you're the only one who can save us," Slocum said, changing his tack. The sense of the argument got through to Caleb.

"They're takin' a terrible shellacking," he said.

"The horses." Slocum had started to join Tewksbury and the others when Caleb shouted out to him.

"Did you find my sister?"

Slocum looked back over his shoulder. His dour expression told Caleb more than he wanted to know. Caleb sagged as he went about the chore Slocum had set for him.

Lead tearing through the air all around, Slocum made his way up to a ditch beside the road, where Tewksbury and two others hunkered down.

"You git her, Slocum?"

"Shooting started before I could get a good look," Slocum said. "We can't stay here much longer. They've got more men than I saw before. Some are in the barn and others are in the house."

"We got a passel of 'em out in that field, too, shootin' at us from the flank."

"How many did you lose?"

Tewksbury spat.

"Four dead, that I know of. Another ten winged. If we don't hightail it mighty soon, all of us'll be dead."

"Caleb is rounding up the horses," Slocum said.

"Is that where the coward got off to?"

"He's going to save your bacon," Slocum said. "Try to run back down the road and you'll be giving Cooper his favorite target."

"You were in the army, weren't you? What do you think we oughta do?"

"Keep firing. How's your ammunition holding up?"

"Most of us had a box or two tucked into our pockets, but we been burnin' through it mighty fast just to keep 'em pinned down."

Slocum caught movement out of the corner of his eye, flopped to his belly, aimed and fired. A man creeping onto the roof of the house jumped, lost his footing and slid off the roof to fall heavily to the ground. Slocum got off a second shot at him but missed. The gunman scrambled to the rear of the house for cover.

"They get up on the roof, they'll be shootin' down on us. Good thing we came in 'fore them bastards out in the field got to the trees on either side of the road," Tewksbury said.

Slocum had thought the same thing. Tewksbury had arrived before Blevins had a chance to deploy his men properly. Otherwise, Tewksbury and the ranchers would have ridden into a crossfire that would have left every single one of them dead.

"The only good news is that the men in the barn don't have much of a shot at us," Slocum said. "Keep the house between us and them." Even as he spoke, the men in the field began moving in on their left side. Whoever was in charge must have had military training to organize and command the men so expertly. Slocum knew there were only minutes left before they were all dead unless they began to retreat now.

"Pass the word to the men in the center to retreat," he said. "Keep both sides firing, then have them back up to the road. That'll concentrate us all along the road, but maybe the extra firepower will hold them at bay."

Slocum kept his attention on the house, hoping to catch sight of Cooper. The men inside the house were too canny to do more than poke their rifles through broken windows and take random shots at the attacking ranchers. He was forced to join the fight to slow the men advancing from the field. He watched carefully, and saw one man poke his head up from behind a rock and pull it back real quick. Slocum knew human nature and how men thought. He aimed at a spot to one side and waited. The man had thought to draw fire to the place he had appeared first. Slocum shot him through the head when he chanced a quick look at the side of the rock.

"Hurry it up," Slocum yelled, seeing that Blevins's men were going to make a full charge because they had heard the slackening of fire from the road. The men in the center of Tewksbury's force couldn't fire without hitting their friends. But the flanks fell back and gave all the men the chance to shoot just as Blevins's men launched their attack.

The roar of rifles firing deafened Slocum. He had been in artillery barrages that were quieter. He fired as fast as he could get a cartridge into the chamber and pull the trigger. It didn't matter if he aimed. All he wanted was for a powerful lot of lead to fill the air and keep Blevins's gunmen down.

His ploy didn't work. They ran forward, screaming and shooting as they came. Tewksbury's men did the only thing they could do. They counterattacked. Slocum saw five men die in the span of a few seconds, and he didn't even know to which side they owed their allegiance.

He turned his attention back to the house when he heard a shout from inside.

"Git 'em, kill 'em, boys!" The voice was muffled, but

Slocum clearly saw Blevins and Cooper come out onto the porch.

There was something odd about the way they walked, but Slocum ignored that when he saw his chance and took it. He fired at Cooper and sent the killer's hat flying through the air. Then Blevins swung around, as if to shield his son. Slocum's rifle came up empty or he would have fired a second time at them.

A rifle discharged next to his ear and made his ears ring. Tewksbury stood there and fired frantically, every round finding its target in Matt Blevins's body.

"Die, you son of a bitch. You took my daughter. You die!" Tewksbury tried to plug Cooper, too, but the man had dropped down out of sight on the porch.

"He killed my pa!" Cooper shouted from hiding. "They murdered Old Man Blevins! They shot him in the back! Get 'em. Cut 'em all down where they stand!"

The fusillade that followed filled the air with choking white gunsmoke. Worse, the men who had been guarding the barn poured forth like ants from an anthill. Each and every one of them screamed at the top of his lungs as he ran to avenge Blevins's death.

14

"Run like hell!" Slocum's advice came late. All the ranchers were running as if a pack of mad dogs was snapping at their heels. Slocum whipped out his six-shooter and began firing carefully, reserving a couple rounds. His four shots took down one man and wounded another. Then he was running with the rest of Tewksbury's invasion force.

"Get on out of here, you hear?" Tewksbury was intent on seeing that as many of his friends as possible were on the road and headed for the safety of his ranch. Caleb had done a good job of rounding up their horses. Only a few men had to ride double, but then there ought to have been many spares because of the men who had fallen to Cooper's attack.

"Grab yer horse, Slocum," Tewksbury shouted. "We kin fight 'em another day."

Slocum waved him on. He had come here to kill Cooper and rescue Lydia and had done neither.

"Catch!" Caleb Tewksbury tossed him a rifle. Slocum levered a round into the chamber and was pleased to see that the young man had given him a fully loaded Henry repeater. Without bothering to respond, Slocum dived for cover in the ditch he had used to get close to the Blevins house before. This time he had to avoid being seen by a couple dozen men running from house and barn, firing wildly and sure of their rout.

Slocum chanced a quick look. The disorderly retreat was as complete as it could be. Tewksbury had lost almost a quarter of his men and that many more were bloodied and might not have much determination to keep up the fight. Then Slocum ducked down and started wiggling back.

He worked his way faster to the house and saw that Cooper had ordered everyone in a total attack. If Tewksbury had planned his mission better, they could have lured Cooper and his men into an ambush. As it was, Cooper's men hooted and hollered and shot after the rapidly scattering ranchers. Slocum reached the window where he had shot through before. This time he snaked over the sill and flopped onto the floor. He got to his feet, stepped over the bodies of the men he had put down earlier and made a quick search of the house.

"Lydia!" he called again, hoping she would answer. There might not be a chance to call out any louder—or ever again if Cooper returned. Slocum heard nothing stirring inside. He opened doors and poked into closets but failed to find the auburn-haired woman anywhere. Cooper had hidden her somewhere else.

The men from the field milled around and joined those from the barn and the handful of survivors from the house to congratulate themselves. Slocum knew he had only a few seconds before Cooper and some of his lieutenants would come back into the house, but something had been worrying at him like a burr under a saddle blanket.

Working onto the porch on his belly, he went to Matt Blevins's body. Slocum grabbed a handful of shirt and heaved, rolling the man onto his back. None of the bullets had entered Blevins from the front but three had exited, leaving big wet holes. Rolling him back, Slocum saw that Blevins had taken four rounds in the back. One bullet hole was much smaller than the other three—the three that had gone all the way through the body.

"Cooper, you son of a bitch. You shot your own pa in the back!"

Slocum heard Andy Cooper and several others coming and had to retreat into the house. He pressed against a wall, his six-gun out. He had two rounds left and a rifle with six or seven rounds in it.

"We gotta bury your old man, Andy," someone said. "Damn shame the way Tewksbury cut him down."

"Shot him in the back with that rifle of his," Cooper said. "You can see the holes."

"Four times, yep," said another. "He never had a chance. Shot in the back every last damn time!"

Slocum wanted to blurt out that Blevins had been dead when he and Cooper went out onto the porch. Cooper had been supporting his father's weight—his dead weight. It only appeared that Tewksbury had killed Blevins, leaving Cooper in the clear. Slocum wasn't sure what the Blevins spread was worth, but it had to be a pretty penny. Now it was all Andy Cooper's.

"Come on in and let's have a drink. We can get my pa buried later," Cooper said. "Shootin' up those owlhoots made me work up quite a thirst."

"That the only thing you been doin' to work up a thirst?" asked another henchman. Slocum tensed. They had to be joking about what Cooper had done to Lydia.

"I need to tend to that some more, but later. I'm tuckered out right now. You didn't let anything happen to her during the gunfight, did you?"

"I told you that you could trust me, Andy," the voice said. "She's got all the comforts of home back there in the barn, even if the room's a mite small."

"That's not all that's small 'bout her," Cooper said. "We were—"

The door opened and Cooper started to go inside. Slocum cocked his six-gun and aimed it for the spot where Cooper's head would appear. But the man stopped.

"What's that? Hell, can't you figger it out yourself?" Cooper closed the door and went to tend to whatever problem had come up. Slocum lowered his six-shooter and tried to work through his dilemma. He had little firepower and was in the midst of the enemy camp. Cooper had dozens of men all het up from winning a gunfight, but killing Cooper had been only half of the reason he had come to the Blevins ranch. Rescuing Lydia had to account for something.

And he knew Cooper was keeping her captive in the barn. He might escape with his own hide intact, but that wasn't the way John Slocum lived his life. He drifted through the house like smoke on the wind and found a rear window. He knocked out the glass and dropped to the ground. He took a deep breath and looked at the twenty yards between the house and barn. It might as well have been the distance from San Francisco to New York. Boldness would work for him where stealth no longer would.

Straightening, walking as if he were a man being told to go fetch something from the barn, he began walking. Every step he took might be his last. He tried not to cringe at the sound of Cooper's gang all around the house. But he didn't turn so any could get a look at his face. He didn't speed up or slow down. The steady pace brought him to the barn door. Only then did he betray his edginess by ducking fast through the door into the cool interior.

"Lydia?" He called her name softly. If Cooper had tied her up, she wouldn't be able to come to him. If Cooper had left guards with her, Slocum didn't want to lure them out until he was sure how many there were. He cocked his head to one side and strained to hear the slightest reply. Nothing. Moving fast, he checked the stalls and went to the rear, where the tack room and a storage room both promised safe places for Cooper to leave the woman.

The tack room stood empty except for the strong scent of leather and saddle soap. Slocum had started to lift the latch on the storage room when he heard men coming. He looked around and saw a ladder leading up to the hayloft. Scrambling as fast as he could without making overt noise, he had barely reached the loft when Cooper came in, flanked by four henchmen.

"You want some help, Andy?"

"Get outta here before I whup you good," Cooper said, obviously joshing.

"You deserve a little reward after all that's happened today." The man shook his head sadly. "Imagine killin' Old Man like that. Shot him in the back."

"They're animals," Cooper said. "Wait outside and keep a sharp lookout for Slocum. I looked for his body and didn't see it."

"Aw, Andy, from all you've told us 'bout him, he's a yellowbelly and probably ran like a scalded dog when he got the chance. He's with the rest of 'em over at Tewksbury's place."

"We'll mosey on over there when Larsen and his boys get here. Ought to be anytime." •

Slocum tensed at this. Cooper and "Shotgun" Larsen had been thick as thieves down in Texas. If there was any killer more inclined to shoot a man in the back than Andy Cooper, it was Larsen. Mention that he was arriving soon told Slocum the battle that Tewksbury had just lost would be fought—and his side would lose again. Between Cooper and Larsen there wasn't likely to be anyone left.

If Cooper could shoot his own father in the back, expecting mercy from him in a gunfight was out of the question. This set Slocum's pulse racing. Cooper held Lydia captive and it was obvious what he was going to do. It didn't matter to Slocum that Cooper had four henchmen waiting for him outside the barn. He would plug the owlhoot and put an end to his putrid life, even if it meant putting Lydia in more danger.

Slocum started to shinny down the ladder but stopped when a half dozen men came into the barn to tend their horses. Getting past them wasn't possible. Slocum silently retreated to the loft and looked around. A broken board at the rear of the loft, above the storage room, afforded him hope of getting down without being seen. Slocum pulled the board free and peered down into a narrow stone chimney that had been sealed after the storeroom had been added. Slocum saw he couldn't fit easily, and taking the rifle with him was out of the question. The fit was too tight. He dropped his gunbelt and clutched the ebony handle of the Colt. Two shots. That was enough to end Cooper's life.

Slocum pried loose another board, took a deep breath and then slid down the chimney. He fell five feet and then realized he had made a terrible mistake. He found himself wedged into the chimney so tightly he couldn't move. His arms were stretched above his head, his six-shooter clutched in his right hand. He wiggled, then struggled with increasing alarm when it became obvious he was unable to drop any farther and was unlikely to get back up the narrow chute.

The sounds coming from the room made his attempts to free himself even more frantic.

"Take off that blouse, bitch," Cooper said. "I want to see you naked."

"No," came Lydia's defiant voice. "I won't do it—oh!"

Slocum heard cloth tearing and imagined he saw buttons flying across the small room, ricocheting off the walls like pearl bullets.

"Nice," Cooper said. "Real nice titties you got. What would you say if I licked them?"

"No, you wouldn't!" The gasp and moan from Lydia told Slocum that Cooper was doing just that. "Oh, your mouth," the woman gasped out. "You're sucking my nipples. I'm on fire all over."

"I'll set you on fire even more. Get out of that skirt. I want you buck naked."

"Make me!"

Slocum heard another ripping sound. Had Cooper torn off her skirt? There were small rustling sounds as if he tossed aside her skirt and worked to get her frilly undergarments pulled down around her ankles. The memory of that auburn patch between her legs, the musky odor and the heat boiling from within made Slocum struggle even harder to get free. All he succeeded in doing was creating more horror for himself. A stone came free from the chimney just under his chin and caught between his chest and the rocks lower down, causing pain every time he took a breath. Worse, he got a limited view of the storeroom and what Cooper was doing.

Patches of naked flesh swept past his narrow peephole, and then he got a full view of Cooper holding both of Lydia's wrists in one hand as he forced her down on a table and fondled her breasts with the other. He moved from one succulent mound to the other, toying with the increasingly taut nip on one and then licking at it noisily before repeating the assault on the other.

"You're 'bout the tastiest thing I ever sampled," Cooper said.

"D-don't sample lower," Lydia got out. It was as if she had given Cooper an idea that would never have occurred to him.

His free hand parted her thighs. Slocum caught sight of that auburn-furred paradise Lydia had shared with him. But she wasn't sharing with Cooper. He was taking. The outlaw moved his mouth across her naked belly to the tangled patch. She gasped aloud when he applied his mouth to her most intimate region.

She began to struggle, but his grip was too powerful to escape. He held her wrists easily with his right hand while he moved his left under her buttocks. Lydia arched upward, cramming herself into his face as he did something to her Slocum wasn't able to see.

"That's what I like," Cooper said. "Cooperation."

Slocum saw Lydia kicking and struggling as the man applied his mouth to her once more. Slocum tensed his shoulders and tried to force more stones in the chimney loose so he could move. If he could get his right hand down, he could thrust his six-gun through the hole and shoot Cooper. It seemed fitting that he would shoot Cooper in the back while he was raping a woman. But as hard as Slocum tried, he couldn't budge any more stones.

"Turn over. I want to take you like a dog," Cooper said. Lydia tried to kick him, but his hand caught her ankle and he somehow deftly flipped her over. Slocum caught a glimpse of her breasts as she ended up facedown on the table, bent in such a way that she presented her behind to Cooper.

"So smooth. Smooth and silky and tasty." Cooper fondled her buttocks and then began kissing them. When Lydia tried to rise up, he pushed her flat on the table.

"Oh, you're crushing my breasts."

"Excites you, don't it?" he said with glee. "Admit it, everything I'm doin' to you is exciting. Say it. Say it!"

He swatted her taut, naked behind.

"No, I'll never say anything like that."

"Say it!" He applied his hand again. Slocum saw the pink outline of Cooper's hand appear on her snowy white flesh. Lydia wiggled and struggled but her legs parted a little, giving Cooper all the encouragement he needed. "I thought so. You want more than my hand, don't you?"

"No, yes!"

Cooper thrust his finger into her. From the way his shoulder muscles rippled, he was moving his hand around furiously.

Slocum was forced to watch because he couldn't get his six-gun lowered enough to stop Cooper. He kicked a little and the toe of his boot caught an outcropping of stone. Slocum pressed down as hard as he could and managed to scoot upward a fraction of an inch before his toe slipped off the soot-covered rock.

He fell back to where he had been, to watch Cooper having his way with Lydia.

"Yeah, baby, round and smooth and so inviting. That's what you're doin', isn't it? Inviting me to do some more to you?"

"Please," sobbed out Lydia. "Take your fingers out."

"All right. I'll do that because you asked all polite." For a moment Slocum thought Cooper was going to let the woman go. Then he saw Cooper discard his gunbelt and undo the fly of his jeans. Cooper stepped up, gripped the woman's hips and pulled her back, forcing her body into the curve of his groin. Lydia cried out as Cooper entered her from behind. The outlaw grunted with pleasure and began stroking back and forth.

Slocum closed his eyes to keep from watching, but he heard the sounds as plainly as if he were in the room with them. He opened his eyes, blinked out soot and watched in fascination, like a bird captivated by a snake, as Cooper finished in a rush.

"Oh, Andy, that was so good," Lydia said.

For a moment Slocum thought his ears betrayed him. Lydia's tone wasn't that of a woman who had just been raped. It was that of a woman who had gotten from her lover what she wanted most.

Lydia turned over on the table and lifted her feet to the edges, then lewdly spread her knees to expose herself to Cooper's lustful gaze.

"You got any more steam in that engine?" she asked.

"You always bring out the best in me, Lydia," he said. Cooper moved forward, bent over and kissed the woman. Or did she kiss him? To Slocum it was obvious that Lydia was giving as good as she got.

And then Cooper was moving between the woman's legs, facing her this time. The anger Slocum felt at risking his life to rescue her powered his feet enough to find the small stone ledge once more. He kicked down and propelled himself a few inches up the chimney. This was enough to relieve the pressure on his chest and let him breathe more freely.

To his relief, the butt of his pistol also rested on a ledge. Pulling upward, using the six-gun as a lever and pushing with his toe, he got free. He worked up the rest of the way to finally drop into the hay in the loft, filthy with soot and burning with anger.

Lydia was in cahoots with Cooper. Worse, they were lovers. Slocum knew then that she had ignored him when he had seen her crossing the pastureland because she was too intent on meeting Cooper. Why Cooper hadn't wanted her to cry out and alert the three drunken cowboys was something Slocum could only guess at. It might have been part of their playacting, her pretending to be the helpless captive and Cooper the bold conqueror.

Slocum was too disgusted to want to find out, much less care for the answer.

He found a stack of rags and wiped the soot off himself the best he could. As he finished, he heard Cooper and Lydia below between the stalls. He looked down at them, arms laced as they left the barn. Slocum pointed his six-shooter at them. He had two shots left. The hammer came back, but he couldn't decide who got the first shot. He hesitated too long making his decision. They left the barn and were joined by Cooper's four henchmen. Loud calls, and others rushed up.

"Larsen, you old son of a whore," Cooper called cheerfully. "Good to see your ugly face again."

Slocum sagged back into the hay. Cooper's reinforcements had arrived. Deadly killers to fight Tewksbury's peaceable ranchers.

He had to let Tewksbury know—about the gunmen he faced, if not about his treacherous daughter who had sold out body and soul to his most deadly adversary.

15

"You look like you been rode hard and put away wet, Slocum," John Tewksbury said as he stared up at Slocum. "Leastways, you stole yerse'f a nice-lookin' horse." The way the man looked at him told Slocum he wasn't merely making chin music but wanted to know if his daughter was all right. Slocum wasn't sure how he was going to answer that.

"They owed it to me," Slocum said, dismounting. It had been a long night. He had hidden in the barn for several hours while the festivities surrounding Larsen's arrival and Cooper's victory over the ranchers dragged on. Eventually, enough whiskey had been downed to make even the most attentive guard sloppy. Slocum had walked past one sentry passed out at the corral and had his pick of the horses. He hoped he had chosen Cooper's horse—or at least Larsen's—but all he wanted was a horse strong enough to carry him away from the Blevins ranch and back here.

Slocum looked around the small bivouac in front of the Tewksbury house and saw tiny knots of men hunched over cooking fires. There wasn't a whole lot of merriment. What surprised him, though, was the number of men who had stayed. After such a crushing defeat most ranchers would have returned to their spreads, tails between their legs like whipped dogs, and worked hard at thinking up excuses for what had gone wrong and promises to make to Andy Cooper so they wouldn't be on the wrong end of his wrath.

"Spit it out, Slocum. You know what I want to hear."

Slocum hesitated. He had no reason to hurt Tewksbury, but the sight of Lydia with Cooper had caused him considerable upset. And worse, he had risked his life for a no-account whore.

"I couldn't get to her," Slocum said carefully. "But she's not hurt. Cooper is keeping her safe and sound."

"Why hasn't he sent a ransom demand? The varmint ain't so dumb as to think I wouldn't give him anything he wanted fer Lydia's return."

"There'll be a price to pay eventually," Slocum said. "It's just not now." He looked around at the yard and the dozen fires sputtering there. "Doesn't look like you lost many of them."

"The only ones I lost are dead. We gotta git 'em back from Cooper so's we kin bury 'em."

"He got a dozen or so men to reinforce him this afternoon," Slocum said. "A real stone killer name of Larsen."

"Shotgun Larsen?" Tewksbury shook his head. "I heard of him when we was in Texas. If Cooper shoots 'em in the back, Larsen does the same, only with a shotgun so's there won't be any chance he'll miss."

"He's the one," Slocum said. "You're going to need a small army to go up against killers of his water. Send word to the sheriff over in Prescott and have him bring a posse. Even better, alert the commander at Fort Apache and get a company of cavalry troopers here. Even forty or fifty soldiers might not be enough to stop Cooper."

"He's a bad one, but with his pa shot like that, he ain't gonna stop till he's got revenge."

"Cooper shot his own father in the back, then dragged the body out to make it look like you killed him. Matt Blevins was dead before he came out on that porch."

"Son of a bitch," Tewksbury said, slapping his thigh. A

small dust cloud rose. He wiped his hand on his vest. "There ain't nuthin' that owlhoot won't do, is there?"

Slocum knew exactly how far Cooper had already gone, but he said nothing. Tewksbury would give up and ride out of the Tonto Basin if he thought his own daughter was with Andy Cooper of her own accord.

Slocum wondered what Tewksbury might do if he ever found out that Lydia had been sleeping with Tom Graham, too.

"You need a better plan than riding straight into their guns," Slocum said. "More men would go a ways toward a victory, too."

"Cain't afford to lose another fight, kin I? Well now, I got word out to a dozen other ranches. Most of them ought to show up by noon tomorrow with ammunition, maybe explosives and fifty or more men willing to fight. Turned out there was fewer men who'd taken a likin' to Old Man Blevins than I thought. And the ones what remember Andy, they're willin' to join up."

"To split up both the Graham and Blevins spreads?" Slocum asked. He saw Tewksbury react enough to know this was the bait used to lure allies.

"Won't do them varmints much good if all of 'em is dead."

"What do you get out of all this?"

"My daughter," Tewksbury said, sounding as if he meant it. "Turn in, Slocum, git all rested up. Tomorrow's gonna determine the future of this whole territory."

Slocum noticed that Tewksbury hadn't said anything about more careful planning. If he didn't have some clever attack mapped out with all the ranchers behind him, he'd be right about the fight ending the feud in the Basin.

"He's not been here in years," Tewksbury said, "so's I figger he'll think this is a good way to come." The grizzled man pointed out the valleys and ravines in the rolling pastureland. "Him and his gang'll come ridin' up from their

place and have to funnel down into that there ravine. We hit
'em from both sides. Real purty strategy, ain't it, Slocum?"

"Only if he doesn't split his men into two groups, one
riding down the ravine and the other coming from behind
those hills. You ought to have a scout or two posted a couple miles off to warn you."

"I need every single gun I kin muster. He ain't bright
enough to think like that. After he won so easy at his place,
he'll reckon he kin do it all over again out here. He's wrong."

Slocum worried about the blind spot behind Tewksbury's left flank. The men along the right side of the ravine
wouldn't be in position to support or attack if Cooper
caught those on the left bank from front and back.

"You sure all these gents are loyal to you?" Slocum had
to admit the hundred or more men gathered provided an
impressive number. Whether they could fight was one
thing. Whether they could fight shoulder to shoulder like
soldiers with the lead flying at them was something else.

"I kin git 'em into position and out again, if it comes to
that," Tewksbury assured him. "But I'm mighty worried
about Lydia. You think Cooper might bring her along, as a
shield? I couldn't order any kind of attack if he was hidin'
behind her skirts."

"He won't do that," Slocum said. From what he had seen
of Cooper and Lydia together, the outlaw wanted to impress
Lydia with how brave he was. To do that she might be watching from some safe vantage, but Cooper would want her far
enough away so he could cut and run, if the need arose. He
might even indulge himself in some savagery that wouldn't
be seen by her; then he could go and have his way with her.

Slocum found himself grinding his teeth together. He
had taken a fancy to Lydia. Maybe not for a long spell, but
the time he had been here he had liked her. Finding out she
slept with her pa's worst enemies revealed a dark current
flowing under her bright smile that Slocum had not
guessed was there. Misjudging her so completely rankled
as much as anything.

"I got to git the men into position. Caleb's offered to be the decoy and lead the lambs to the slaughter."

"Caleb?"

"He wants to git his sister back safe and sound, too. We're family, Slocum. Blood's thicker'n water." With that, Tewksbury rode off shouting to other ranchers and getting them split into two roughly equal forces, one for each side of the deep, rugged, rocky ravine where he thought he could trap Cooper.

Slocum kept eyeing the distant ridge. One more gun wasn't going to matter. He wished Caleb had been available to go scout that distant ridge, but Slocum couldn't fault the young man for his willingness to go along with this cockamamie battle plan even trained soldiers weren't likely to execute properly. All it took was one man to get buck fever and fire early to warn Cooper away from the ambush. Even if everything went well, Slocum knew it would be a fight. Tewksbury had not bothered with a plan to bottle up Cooper and his men. If they started taking serious casualties, all Cooper had to do was retreat the way he had come.

But that distant ridge—Cooper need only bring a dozen men over it to completely destroy Tewksbury's strategy.

"Git ready, boys. There's Caleb signalin' he's got Cooper followin' him!"

"Tewksbury, I'm going to the other side, to scout the ridge," Slocum called, but the rancher was too caught up in playing general. Tewksbury shouted orders that made no sense, but that hardly mattered since no one was paying him any attention. The ranchers knew what had to be done and were getting ready for Cooper to ride into the ravine like a cow down the chute in a slaughterhouse.

Slocum stood in his stirrups and shielded his eyes when he saw a solitary rider trotting along at the foot of the hill he worried most about. He grabbed his field glasses from his saddlebags and peered into them. His heart leapt when he saw that it was a woman.

"Lydia!"

A more careful look told him this was some other woman, older and bigger than the petite Lydia Tewksbury and sporting midnight dark hair that escaped here and there from under her hat.

"Tewksbury," he called, but the man had ridden away. Slocum got his mare down the steep ravine embankment and found a path up the other slope. He had to warn the woman away from the battle. How she had ridden out across the Basin today, at this precise time was something he didn't want to think on. Coincidences like that could prove deadly. Worse, Cooper might spot her and not be lured into Tewksbury's trap.

Slocum lost sight of her in the rolling hills. He struggled to get to the top of a low rise and then forgot all about the solitary woman. His worst fear had been realized. He swung in the saddle and looked down the ravine where Caleb galloped hard, a half dozen men following him. A half dozen! The rest of Cooper's back-shooting murderers attacked in exactly the way Slocum had feared they might. More than fifty armed and ready outlaws crested the hill, then rushed forward.

"It's a trap!" Slocum shouted. Seeing that his warning fell on deaf ears, he drew his rifle and began firing, hoping to get the attention of the men on the left bank. They would be trapped between the overwhelming firepower from Cooper's attack and the sheer drop into the ravine. The front line of Cooper's force appeared at the base of the hill where Slocum stood watch. Slocum fired methodically and knocked a horse out from under one of Cooper's men. Then the rest were out of Slocum's rifle range and rushed on to attack the men forming Tewksbury's left flank.

Slocum swung his horse around and cut back at an angle to get in front of the horde of men closing fast on the left flank.

"Behind you. They're coming from behind you!" he shouted. He got off a couple more shots that accomplished nothing. The men Tewksbury had strung out along the left bank of the ravine thought they were hearing only the reports of their own rifles—until hot lead began cutting them down.

Someone turned and saw the danger, but they had no cover from a rear attack. The men on the far side of the ravine were unable to give supporting fire without shooting through their own ranks. But they did anyway. Slocum cringed as hot lead winged over from the other bank, some of it killing allies and the rest wasted.

"Get 'em, men. No quarter. *Dequello!*" Cooper called.

Slocum heard the voice and knew the Mexican order that had been given at the Alamo. No quarter. He slowed his wild gallop and turned more toward Andy Cooper. There was nothing he could hope to do by joining Tewksbury's men in death. But there might be one last gift he could give the world. Kill Andy Cooper.

Slocum swung the rifle to his shoulder as his horse ran into the ranks of Cooper's men. He squeezed off a shot that missed Cooper by a country mile. His next shot was hardly closer, but the third one he managed to get off just as his horse was straining forward and not bouncing him all over the meadow. He was pleased to see Cooper recoil and grab for his right side. Slocum's bullet had drawn blood. He had hoped for a clean kill, but this was enough for the moment. It forced Cooper to fall back and let his men advance without him shouting encouragement.

Not that any of them needed it. Shotgun Larsen rode near the front of the tidal wave washing over Tewksbury's flank. His sawed-off, double-barreled weapon roared repeatedly, and the loads of heavy buckshot tore savage paths through men who had only seconds before thought they were going to win this battle. From the corner of his eye Slocum saw one man's head explode as Larsen loosed both barrels at almost point-blank range. Then Larsen galloped past before the man's headless body hit the ground.

Slocum saw that he no longer had a clear shot at Cooper. The owlhoot fell back and let his men form a shield between him and Slocum.

But Slocum found himself suddenly occupied when he heard his name called out.

"Slocum, you miserable sheep-lovin'—" The rest of Shotgun Larsen's imprecation was drowned out by the thunder of dozens of rifles being fired—all at Tewksbury's men.

Slocum bent low so that Larsen's buckshot missed his head. Hot stabs on his side told him that at least two of the shotgun pellets had grazed him, though. A little wobbly from the pain, Slocum lifted his rifle and fired. He hit someone, but it wasn't Larsen. Then he was sliding down the steep embankment into the ravine. He heard the report of a shotgun and felt his horse melt under him. When he hit the rocky bottom, he knew his mare was dead from a double blast of double-ought buck.

He lay on the gravelly stream bottom and waited. Above him the roar of death-giving rifles and pistols went on unabated. Tewksbury's men had dropped their weapons and tried to escape, only to find no way to retreat. Too many of them had been shot down by their own side and by the ranchers stretched along the right-hand side of the ravine. Slocum lifted his head a little and saw bodies littering the ground all around him. Without moving too much, he slid his Colt Navy free of its holster, cocked it and waited.

It didn't take Larsen long to find a path down into the ravine. He wanted to stand over Slocum's dead body and gloat. Between half-opened eyelids, Slocum watched the killer ride up. Larsen puffed up his chest and looked like he was going to give voice to a long, loud cry of triumph, like some jungle animal.

Slocum never gave him the chance. He rolled onto his side, winced at the pain from the two creases in his hide, aimed and fired. The bullet caught Larsen just under the chin and knocked his head back. Larsen fell, but his feet caught in his stirrups. His horse reared, then tore out at a gallop, going past Slocum and up the ravine, its grisly cargo bouncing from side to side. Slocum pushed up to one elbow and flopped over in time to see Larsen finally fall free of his horse.

"See you in hell, Shotgun," Slocum said. Moving painfully, Slocum got to his feet and immediately dived for the bank of the deep ravine to avoid the fire from Cooper's men now occupying the left bank.

Sporadic fire came from those on the right side, but Slocum suspected most of them had seen the handwriting on the wall and hightailed it. Twice now John Tewksbury had lost a major fight with Blevins and his son, Andy Cooper.

"Kill 'em, kill 'em all, men!" Cooper shouted encouragement from just above Slocum.

Craning his neck around, Slocum caught sight of the outlaw pointing to the far side of the ravine. Slocum got off a shot and nicked Cooper's wrist. Luckily for him, Cooper thought the round came from the other side of the ravine. Otherwise, if Cooper had ordered all the gunfire turned downward, Slocum would have been cut to bloody ribbons.

Realizing that his hatred for the man was clouding his judgment, Slocum began edging along the ravine wall, hunting for some way to climb up the far side and get help from Tewksbury and his men. Cooper wasn't inclined to give up and begin his second celebration in as many days. He kept his men firing at anything moving on the right side of the ravine.

Slocum found escape in an unlikely place. Shotgun Larsen's horse ambled back, nudged at its dead rider and then started pawing the ground as if it wanted to bury him on the spot. Slocum made his way to the horse, glad that most of Tewksbury's men had already retreated. This caused Cooper's gunmen to eye the horizon and not look down at their feet. He swung into the saddle and stayed low, urging the horse to walk up the ravine, away from the gunfire. This proved easy enough, although the horse shied occasionally because of the stench of blood. Slocum tried to press his bandanna into first one and then the other of his new wounds, but he couldn't apply enough pressure on either to stanch the flow.

The horse kept moving, and this suited Slocum as he got a little dizzy. He found himself grabbing onto the pommel to keep from toppling to the ground. For a few minutes, Slocum rode without knowing what he did. Then he snapped alert when he realized there was nothing but rolling grassy meadow around him. He sat upright, groaned at the pain and then looked around. It took several seconds for him to realize the ravine that had flowed red with the blood of Tewksbury's supporters lay far behind.

"Antietam," Slocum muttered. The fight between Tewksbury and Cooper had turned into a new Antietam with the streams running with blood. The difference this time was that Cooper had not taken the casualties Tewksbury had. There was a clear victor—and it wasn't going to be good for Slocum to stay in the Tonto Basin much longer.

But he almost fell off the horse as weakness hit him again. He had lost more blood than he thought. Both wounds left by the pellets from Larsen's deadly shotgun continued to ooze, and nothing he did stopped the flow.

"Take me outta here. Larsen shot me up good," Slocum said to the horse, "but you can make it all good by getting me the hell out of here."

The horse let out a moist snort, and Slocum couldn't tell if the animal was agreeing or telling him there wasn't any way it would cooperate with the man who had killed its owner.

The ruckus behind him died down as he rode farther away, but Slocum wasn't sure where he was going. He jerked upright when it occurred to him the only place this horse might know in the Basin was the Blevins barn. Being carried to the heart of Cooper's stronghold would get him killed as sure as rain.

"There," Slocum said, tugging on the reins. "Let's go in that direction." He wasn't too sure where he was going, but north lay danger. With the sun hot on his back, he knew he was riding east. When he came to the road running from the Tewksbury spread to Tom Graham's, he would go south. Might be Tewksbury was still alive and could patch him up. If not, Cooper would take his time burning out Tewksbury and give Slocum that much more time to head to the Sierra Anchas and a hope of safety.

A faint hope, if the Apaches still roamed, but better than any he had if he remained in the Tonto Basin much longer.

The sun was setting, making the shadows in front him stretch forever. Slocum kept his directly in front, but when the sun set, he had to figure some other way to know which direction east lay. In his condition he knew he would likely start riding in a circle. As weak as he was, he would fall off and die. Or ride into some of Cooper's men.

"Road, there's the road," he said. The sight of the double-rutted dirt path sent a thrill through him that kept him going. "To the right. Turn right and go to Tewksbury's." He spoke aloud to keep it all straight in his jumbled mind. A mistake now because his lost concentration would be fatal.

Deep down inside Slocum wondered if it wasn't already too late for him. Then he hardened and resolve set in. He wasn't going to die. He was going to live and make sure Andy Cooper was planted out in some meadow far from his murdered father's grave.

"Lydia." The woman's name and flashes of how he had last seen her with Cooper galvanized him. He sat straighter and was firmer with the horse as he set it trotting southward.

Slocum had ridden only a mile when he heard hoof-beats on the road behind him. He doubted anyone sympathetic to him was likely to be out after sundown, and he tried to turn the horse off the road. The horse bolted and sent Slocum flying. He crashed to the ground and lay stunned. Through blurred eyes he saw the silhouettes of three riders approaching him rapidly.

"You see that horse, Andy?" called one rider. "That was Larsen's horse. I'd know it anywhere."

"That sure as hell wasn't Shotgun riding it. I found his body in the ravine."

"Who stole his horse?"

"Let's find out," Andy Cooper sad. "Then we kin have some fun with 'im!"

Slocum tried to draw his six-shooter to defend himself but couldn't move. As the trio of riders neared, Slocum collapsed, helpless.

16

"You hear something?" Andy Cooper asked.

"Just a horse ahead of us. Not galloping, just walking away, no big hurry."

"I heard something around here," Cooper said. Slocum craned his neck up and fought to get his six-gun pointed in Cooper's direction. His strength fled and he collapsed face-down. "There. I heard it again."

"I didn't hear it, Andy. Honest."

"Might be a rabbit out there," Cooper said. "Let's do some scouting."

"What about the horse?"

"If it's not in a big hurry to leave, why bother with it? There's a passel of riderless horses since the fight today."

"We whupped 'em good, didn't we?"

"What a bunch of cowards," Cooper said. "They lit out so fast I couldn't even see their scared faces."

"Cowards," his companion agreed.

"You look on the far side of the road. I'll—"

Cooper bit off his order when Larsen's horse suddenly burst from where it had been grazing and galloped away. Both men chased after it, giving Slocum a chance to prop himself up and watch them departing. It wasn't going to be much of a respite because the horse was likely to be caught in a few minutes. That meant Slocum had to act fast.

He forced himself to his feet and staggered along the road leading to the Graham house. There wasn't likely to be anyone there, unless Murphy had turned squatter and claimed it for himself. Slocum fought to put one foot in front of the other and keep moving, until he fell again. He heard Cooper and his henchman behind him, arguing over where the rider who had been on Larsen's horse might have gotten off to.

Slocum saw the dark bulk of Tom Graham's house ahead. He could find a place to hide in the house. If he stayed out in plain sight, Cooper would finish the job started at the battle across the ravine. In his state, Slocum knew he had scant chance of escaping Cooper's search, but lying in the yard in front of the house for God and everyone to see wasn't the way to stay alive.

He gritted his teeth and fought each step up to the porch. Falling hard, he threw his full weight against the front door. It didn't budge. He reached down and caught the latch, tugging upward hard. It didn't budge. He tried again, with no result. With the suddenness of a gallows trapdoor opening, he went sprawling onto the floor. Slocum looked up and saw a woman.

"You . . . I saw you earlier. I tried to warn you 'bout the fight," Slocum said.

"Did you?"

"Did," he said. Slocum fumbled to get his six-shooter out. "Cooper's after me. Kill me if he finds me."

"You fought on Tewksbury's side?"

Slocum was past lying. He nodded.

Then he passed out. When he awoke, he heard angry voices. He groped for his pistol but couldn't find it. Blinking hard, he got a good view of the Graham parlor, but from a curious angle. He finally realized he was stuffed into a cabinet, looking out through beveled glass panels in the top of its door. He didn't remember hiding here, and he certainly didn't remember leaving his six-gun on the table near the door, where the dark-haired woman stood, balled hands on her flaring hips and looking like she was ready to take on the world. Past her, barely visible in the dim light cast by a coal oil lamp on the table by his Colt, stood an angry Andy Cooper.

"I don't care who you are, sir. This is my house and you are not coming inside."

"Outta the way," Cooper said, shoving her to one side. Slocum saw her grab his Colt and tuck it under a fold in her voluminous skirts. She had changed clothes since she'd gone riding this afternoon.

"Watch her," Cooper ordered his partner. "I want to be sure nobody's hidin' here."

"If my husband were still alive, he would never allow this invasion!"

"He's dead, so you shut yer mouth, woman," Cooper said. He went rummaging around the house. Slocum caught his breath when Cooper came toward the cabinet and almost looked him in the eye, but the woman made a protest that captured Cooper's attention again.

"I got reason to think Slocum's around here," Cooper said. "Some of my boys saw him gun down a good friend and steal his horse."

"I don't know who you mean. And look in the barn. All the horses there are Graham horses with our brand."

"I got the horse," Cooper said. "I want the rider."

"Then you had better go look somewhere else for him, because he is not here."

Slocum started when Cooper grabbed the woman by the throat and forced her back against the wall. He tried to open the cabinet door and found it locked on the outside, but the woman didn't need his help. Cooper held her by the throat, but she held Slocum's six-gun in such a way that she could blow off Cooper's manhood if he pressed the issue.

"Let me go," she said, her voice choked.

"Let her be, Andy. You looked 'round the house and he ain't here. I figger he fell off his horse and is out along the road somewhere. You know they said he was hurt something fierce."

Cooper released her and she moved the gun back into the folds of her skirt. Cooper never realized how close he had come to spending the rest of his life as a gelding.

"You come across John Slocum, you let me know and I'll see that you get something good, Mrs. Graham."

"Good night, sir," she said. Cooper laughed and followed his henchman out onto the porch. Slocum saw Cooper order the man to scout around the house while he waited on the porch.

The woman kicked the door shut and barred it, but made no move to come to the cabinet. Slocum knew she waited for the two to ride away. He heaved a sigh of relief at her caution. And then he spilled out onto the floor of her parlor when the latch was unexpectedly opened.

"You're Slocum?" she asked. She trained his own pistol on him, her hand steady. He thought she was probably no stranger to firearms and could hardly miss at this range even if she wasn't.

"John Slocum, like Cooper said. We go back a ways, him and me."

"To Texas?"

"He shot my partner in the back. From what I've seen, his habits haven't improved any since then."

"You were with Tewksbury. I heard him mention the name. He thought highly of you."

"Glad someone does." Slocum sat up, and dizziness hit him. He keeled over, his head resting against a love seat.

"You are shot up," she said. Slocum couldn't summon enough energy to speak. "Let me get you into the bedroom where I can patch you up."

"Obliged," he croaked out, but he found himself unable to help her by standing. His legs folded under him. To his surprise, she had no trouble supporting him. He knew then how he had gotten stuffed into the cabinet. She had wrestled him inside by herself.

"Lie down. Let me get some hot water and bandages. Heaven knows, there are enough bandages around. Tom was always getting himself shot up in one scuffle or another."

Slocum couldn't even roll over. Mrs. Graham returned and began tugging gently at the shirt glued onto his side. She had the strength to carry him but the gentleness to peel away the blood-soaked shirt. He gasped once and then stoically watched as she worked with grim efficiency cleaning the two buckshot wounds, then sewing them up with needle and thread.

"There," she said. "That'll get you back into the pink before you know it. You were lucky the lead shot didn't go into you. I'm not good at digging it out."

"You did just fine," Slocum said. "I've got something else to thank you for."

"Something else?"

"You didn't turn me over to Cooper."

"He was the kind my husband would have invited to dinner."

"Tewksbury and Tom Graham were enemies," Slocum said.

"They were, but that doesn't mean John and I are." She smiled almost wickedly and said, "We were lovers."

Slocum didn't know what to say. Lydia and Tom Graham had been lovers, also. Did either pair know of the other?

"John's lost interest in me now that Tom's dead. I thought that might be what would happen. He thought he was getting revenge on Tom by sleeping with me."

"What were you getting out of it?"

"Satisfaction," she said. "I never loved Tom. And he started treating me worse and worse, until he finally didn't bother coming to my bed. That was fine with me."

"He had another woman?" Slocum ventured this to see what Mrs. Graham knew of her husband and Lydia Tewksbury's amorous adventures.

"I am sure he did, but all I cared was that he ignored me even more. I liked that."

"Cooper might be back. I'd better get out of here or you'll find yourself in big trouble."

"Stay put, Mr. Slocum," she said, pushing him back. "I'm not the kind to waste good work sewing up a man only to have him go get himself killed. Rest up. You need to get your strength back."

"You don't have to do this," he said.

"For John, I do. One last thank-you. I don't see him staying alive too much longer without your help."

"Kill Cooper and the fight's over," Slocum said.

"Yes," she said. "And with Tom no longer involved, that will cause the entire Tonto Basin to settle down. Frankly, I am sick of this place. Too many bad memories."

Slocum started to answer, but the sleep of complete exhaustion overtook him. He awoke to the sunlight slanting in through the bedroom window and the smell of cornbread baking. Although still a little shaky, he sat up, got his feet over the side.

"Don't go straining yourself," Mrs. Graham said, coming in with a tray heaped with food, including the cornbread. Slocum's mouth watered at the sight and smell.

"The only way I'll strain myself is to overeat."

"You lost a considerable amount of blood. Don't be shy eating that calf liver."

As Slocum ate, he studied the woman. She sat quietly in a chair, watching him. She was a little taller than average and well built. Her coal black hair was pulled back and held by a series of gold clasps, but a few strands had still contrived to escape and form a dark cloud around her head. Eyes like chips of turquoise unflinchingly looked at him. She was no shrinking violet. Slocum wondered why she had stayed with Tom Graham if she hadn't loved him and obviously got nothing in return for her loyalty.

"Pickings are slim," she said, as if reading his mind. "Tom was about the only man who could corral me, and when he did, he used a bit too much force."

"You're glad he's dead?"

"I'd be a liar if I said different." Mrs. Graham took the tray from him and set it on the floor beside the bed. "You're looking more fit."

"Feel better," Slocum said. Something about her expression made him wonder what was eating at her. "How can I repay you?"

"Do what a real man does," she said, dropping to her knees beside the bed in front of him. She reached out and worked to unfasten the buttons on his jeans. "You're up to it, aren't you?"

"Looks like I am," Slocum said. The dark-haired woman had unfastened the last button of his fly allowing his manhood to spring out, hard and long and ready.

"Yes, it does," she said, scooting closer. She looked up, her blue-green eyes bright with desire. Then she turned her face down and he felt her hot, wet lips kiss the very tip of his rigid shaft. A shudder passed through Slocum and echoed all the way to his head. He felt dizzy again, but the sensation was different from what he had experienced before.

He sagged back, supporting himself on his elbows and looking down at the top of Mrs. Graham's head as she worked lower on him. Her kisses became more passionate and then she took him entirely into her mouth. He felt her red lips sliding down the sides as her tongue teased the sensitive flesh. As she pulled back, she sucked hard on him and lifted his hips off the bed.

"Back," she said.

"More," Slocum said, reaching down with one hand and guiding her head downward again. She teased with her tongue and scored the sides of his fleshy shaft with her teeth. The suction and lips and the rest of her stimulation, including gently tapping the hairy sac dangling beneath, all threatened to cause Slocum to blow wide open.

But she slowed her pace and didn't resist as he decreased the pressure on the back of her head. She looked up and smiled just a haunting little smile.

"More?"

"More," he said, struggling to bend up so he could reach the buttons of her blouse. He remembered how Cooper had sent Lydia's buttons popping all over the storage room. Slocum slowed his desires and carefully unbuttoned Mrs.

Graham's blouse and then pushed it back to reveal twin mounds of succulent flesh that made his mouth water. He reached around her body, fingers digging into her back, and pulled her forward far enough to put his lips against the taut, cherry-red buttons cresting each breast. As he licked and kissed and sucked, she seemed to soften and flow. She moved up him until she was above him, her breasts dangling down for his delectation. Slocum took one hard upturned nip into his mouth and used tongue and teeth against it as she had done with him down lower.

"More," she said.

"More," he agreed. Slocum reached down and tugged at the woman's skirts, lifting them. He found immediately that she wore nothing under them. She straddled his waist and settled down, taking him in hand and guiding his hardness to her inner warmth. For a moment, she paused. Then Slocum took both her breasts in his hands and began massaging. He caught the blood-engorged nubs between his fingers and twisted them about, using these grips to steer her body lower. He sank fully into her moist, clinging interior.

For a few heartbeats, they stayed like that, neither stirring, both reveling in the building sensations. Then Mrs. Graham began moving up and down, twisting from side to side and tensing her strong inner muscles against Slocum's meaty spire. Slocum felt the surge of pleasure jolt throughout his body and wanted even more. He rocked up and buried his face between her ample breasts, then twisted, throwing her over onto the bed while they were still intimately connected. Her legs came up as she opened herself to him fully.

Slocum began stroking faster and faster. The carnal friction burned away at his control, but he wasn't about to give in to such pleasure yet. Reaching under the woman's body, he grasped her fleshy buttocks and lifted. He kneaded them as he had her breasts, and continued to build up speed. Every stroke took him deeper, gave them both more excitement. And then she cried out, turning and squirming with ecstatic release under him. It felt as if a pile driver crushed his buried organ.

And then he rushed to completion. Slocum might have chalked such a lack of control up to his blood loss, but he knew the real reason. Mrs. Graham was a sexy, knowing, experienced woman who gave as good as she got. He rode out the winds of passion and then settled down atop her. Faces only inches apart, he said, "We ought to have done this sooner."

She looked at him in surprise, then laughed.

"I do declare. You are full of surprises. Maybe that's why I'm so drawn to you."

Slocum studied her face up close and then kissed her to shut up the flow of words. He didn't care to think too much about such things since it always got him into trouble. As it had with Lydia Tewksbury.

After satisfyingly kissing her, Slocum rolled away and got to his feet. She watched as he buttoned himself up.

"You going now?"

Slocum had started to answer when he heard horses in the yard outside. He went to the window and peered through the curtains, squinting into the morning sun.

"Cooper and three of his cronies," Slocum said. He reached for his gunbelt, but the Colt was still missing.

"I'll get it. You better think on how to get away," Mrs. Graham said. "Take any of the horses in the barn."

"What happened to Murphy and the rest of your husband's cowhands?"

She snorted in contempt. "They all lit out when they heard Tom was dead."

She rushed to the front door, grabbed Slocum's six-gun and tossed it to him just as the door opened and Cooper came in without knocking. Slocum closed the bedroom door until he had a crack to peer through. He felt the familiar heft of his Colt Navy and knew he could take care of Andy Cooper with a single shot. But the other three? That would take a powerful lot of luck, and he wasn't sure how many rounds he had left.

"Smelled the food. Feed us, woman," Cooper said, grabbing Mrs. Graham's arm and shoving her toward the kitchen. "You musta been expecting us, to fix up so much."

"I'm getting ready to leave. There's nothing keeping me on this ranch."

"You're right. I'm taking it all. If you're real good to us, I might even let you go."

"After, Andy? She kin go after?"

Slocum poked the barrel of his six-gun through the door and sighted in on Cooper's head.

"There might be time for fun later," Cooper said.

"Later?" Mrs. Graham jerked free from his grip and went to the kitchen to take down plates and put them on the table. Slocum was glad he hadn't eaten there. She would have had to explain the extra plate. "What comes first?"

"Food, then we got to get the rest of my boys together to ride over to the Tewksbury spread. I burn him out and run him off, or maybe I string him up. I wouldn't be averse to seein' John Tewksbury dancing in the air, a rope round his scrawny neck."

"Then you promised, Andy," said another. "You promised we could have the girl."

"Why not?" Cooper said. "I'm done with her. The stupid bitch thinks I'm in love with her. All I want is to know I'm not riding into a trap."

"Belt and suspenders, Andy. That's you. Never take an unnecessary risk."

"I don't know," Cooper said, stroking over Mrs. Graham's hand as she put food on his plate. "This one looks like she'd be mighty dangerous. I like that."

Slocum opened the door a little more to see Mrs. Graham stab him in the hand with a fork. Cooper yelped and backhanded her.

"Don't ever do a thing like that again," Cooper warned.

"You're just like my husband," she said. "My *dead* husband."

"We ain't got time, Andy," said another of his men, uneasily looking at Mrs. Graham and seeing the fight in her. "I'm hungry."

"Eat," Cooper said.

Slocum saw that the threat to the woman had passed, and he closed the bedroom door. He got on his boots, rummaged in a wardrobe and found a shirt, probably Tom Graham's, and slipped into it. He was stiff and sore, but Mrs. Graham had sewn him up well. Dressed, Slocum went out the bedroom window and dropped to the ground in a crouch. He walked in a squat under the windows to the front of the house, where Cooper had left their horses.

Slocum's eyes widened when he saw Cooper's horse. Star. Whether Lydia had given him her prized horse or he had simply taken it hardly mattered. The horse was strong, rested and capable of getting Slocum to the Tewksbury spread fast.

With a quick hop, he swung into the saddle, grabbed up the reins of the other horses and led them away. It wouldn't take Cooper long to find the horses in the Graham barn, but slowing him by even a minute or two might give Tewksbury time to prepare for the attack.

There wasn't any way in hell the rancher could lose a third battle and come out alive. This time it would be more than his life at stake. Lydia and everyone who wasn't backing Cooper would find their lives forfeited, too.

17

Lydia's horse was everything she had claimed. It had heart and galloped farther than Slocum would have thought possible. Even as he was beginning to feel the effect of the hard ride, Star still raced on until the road leading to the Tewksbury house flashed past. Slocum tugged at the reins and turned the horse's wild ride toward the house. The sun was hot on his back as he neared.

Slocum slowed and then stopped to study the house. He had expected to see Caleb on the roof, keeping watch—if Caleb had even survived the debacle at the ravine. There should have been men running around doing chores, getting bunkers ready to ward off an attack Tewksbury must know would follow his last defeat. But he saw nothing. The place was deserted.

He rode closer, then called, "It's me, Slocum. Don't shoot!"

A single rifle barrel had poked out a broken window and pointed directly at him.

"John?"

Slocum sagged. Of all the people he wanted to talk to, Lydia Tewksbury was not one. He looked up when she came from the front door, the rifle clutched in her hands.

She stared at him for a moment, dropped the rifle and

rushed out to throw her arms around Star's neck. The woman hugged her horse hard, causing the tired animal to shy away. She followed, refusing to let the horse go.

"I didn't think I'd see you again. He took you, he took you, Star." Lydia turned her bright eyes up at Slocum and smiled winningly. "Thank you for bringing Star back. Cooper stole—"

"You gave the horse to Cooper," Slocum said flatly. He dismounted and walked around to look down at Lydia. "You and Cooper are lovers. And you gave him the horse and he's the one I stole the horse from."

"There's a dearth of real men around here, John," she said. "You didn't think I was a virgin, did you?"

"I didn't think you were a whore."

Slocum stopped her hand as she tried to slap him.

"Where's your pa? Cooper's getting his men together for an attack." He stared at the flushed, angry woman and couldn't keep from adding, "Cooper's decided to let you pleasure his men. All of them. Seems he got tired of you mighty fast."

"You can't say things like that. You're insulting! You—" She tried to slap him again, and again he stopped her.

"Raped and then murdered," Slocum said savagely. "Those are in your future if Cooper wins. Where's your pa?"

"He . . . he and the men lit out before dawn. They're looking to attack the Blevins ranch and catch Cooper unawares."

"But Cooper believes he has to attack here. You didn't tell him what your pa had in mind, did you? Were you going to welcome Cooper here and help him set fire to your house, your barn, everything?"

"No!"

For once Slocum believed Lydia. It made no sense that Cooper would come here, thinking he was meeting what was left of Tewksbury's allies, if he could lure them to the Blevins ranch and kill them there. Slocum had no doubt Tewksbury would have led his men into another ambush, especially if he was being gulled by his own daughter.

"Are you alone?"

"No, there are a few wounded inside."

"Can they be moved?"

"They are all too badly hurt to move," Lydia said. "Andy wouldn't kill men who are laid up like that. He—"

"He would. He will. The man kills by shooting his betters in the back. He'll see killing everyone in your house as reducing the number who'll heal up and keep fighting him. He'll burn your house and claim all this land as his. He's out to own the entire Tonto Basin."

"I know that," Lydia said in a choked voice. "Andy's got a lot of ambition, but he never said he'd kill everyone."

"If we can't get them to safety, are they able to fight for their lives?" Slocum didn't wait for Lydia to reply. He pushed past her and went into the house. He counted more than a dozen men inside, most of them in a bad way. He walked around, judging how gravely they were hurt.

"You here to give us news on how Tewksbury's doing?" asked a man with both legs splinted.

"He's made a third, bad mistake," Slocum said. "How many of these men can be moved?"

The man with the broken legs laughed ruefully and pointed. "You can see I'm not up to sticking my tail between my legs and running. I can shoot, though, and there're enough rifles around for a small fight."

"It's going to be a big fight." Slocum had awakened the men around him. To his delight most of them looked able to use a six-gun or rifle, even if they weren't up to riding.

"Tewksbury was going to stop Cooper. What went wrong?"

"He doesn't think like a back-shooting son of a bitch," Slocum said. "He thought you'd be safe, and Cooper would fight straight on, man-to-man. Turns out, Cooper wants to kill the wounded and then run Tewksbury out of the Basin, if Tewksbury doesn't get himself ventilated first."

"Jist like John," another said. "Ain't got brains enough fer an itty-bitty li'l bird."

Lydia raged. "Don't say that about my father!" She

stood near the door, listening to everything Slocum said. "He's a good man!"

"You'll be dead men if you don't prepare for the battle," Slocum said. "Those of you who can, get to the windows. Set up the ammo where you can get to it without running around." He looked hard at the man with both legs splinted.

"You do what you have to elsewhere, Slocum," the man said, levering himself up with obvious pain and moving toward a window. "We'll do just fine defending ourselves."

"What are you planning, John?" Lydia asked.

"Not much I can do. What road did your pa take to get to the Blevins spread? I might chase him down and get him to return, but there's not much time for that."

"I don't know how he was going. He and Caleb were chuckling over a secret way to get there. I don't know what they were talking about since the whole Basin is nothing but rolling hills and meadows. How can there be a secret way?"

"Just Tewksbury's way of ginning up support for his crackbrained scheme," Slocum said. "He'll do something stupid like a frontal attack, but it won't be so stupid this time since Cooper's not there. He'll be here burning the house to the ground."

"Quit saying that, John. Please," pleaded Lydia. "Andy's not as bad as you make out. And I . . . I don't believe what you said about him."

"Why don't you get on Star and go find your pa?"

"I don't know where he is!" Lydia almost whined, and tears poured down her cheeks. She looked at Slocum and asked in a choked voice, "Andy said he was going to let his men use me?"

Slocum didn't say a word, because she already knew the answer.

"I'll help everyone get ready for the fight," she said.

"Good. It's not going to be easy."

"You don't have to stay, John. This isn't your fight."

Slocum looked around at the wounded men struggling

to sit up. All of them had their hands on their weapons, ready to fight to the death. There wasn't any way he could run out on bravery like this. He picked up a rifle and began sliding cartridges into the magazine by way of an answer.

Lydia nodded once, then went to the door and opened it. She froze, then slammed it with a cry.

"They're here! That's Cooper riding in front. There're dozens of 'em!"

Lydia's words were almost drowned out by the sharp reports of the attackers' rifles. Hot lead bored through the walls and door and smashed what few shards of glass remained in the windows. Slocum guessed Tewksbury had been proud of those plate-glass windows. It might have cost as much putting real glass in as building the house. Now there were only small fragments to grind under foot.

Slocum took three quick steps and got to the door, held it partly open with the toe of his boot and thrust the rifle out. He squeezed off a shot and sent a rider sprawling, but Slocum usually had a gut instinct about how good a shot he'd just made. This slug had missed. He lowered the muzzle and waited for the man to pop up again at the edge of the porch. Slocum wasn't disappointed. Cooper's henchman thrust his head up like a prairie dog looking for intruders.

Slocum squeezed off the round. This time his gut told him he had made a killing shot.

He didn't have time to savor the skill of his shot or how he had outwitted the man. Too many bullets ripped through the wood around him, forcing him to close the door. He looked around the room and saw that those who had been wounded acquitted themselves well—those who had lived through the first assault on the Tewksbury house.

"We turned the bastards back," crowed the man with both legs in splints. "We'll keep do—"

The man had grown careless and moved so that he presented a clear target from outside. The bullet slashed through his head and killed him instantly.

"Oh, no," Lydia said, watching him slide to the floor. "No, no, this isn't right."

Slocum was too slow grabbing for her. She ran to the door and flung it open, screaming, "Andy, Andy, don't shoot!"

Slocum tackled her in time to keep her from being filled with lead. Lydia struggled under him as he pulled her back into the house. Using the rifle stock, he knocked her back, then got off three quick shots that did nothing, but made him feel better.

"He was going to kill me."

"That's better than what I heard him say he'd do."

"You're horrible!" Lydia curled up and began crying hysterically.

Slocum ignored her and went to the window where the broken-legged man had been posted, in time to shoot at a rider galloping forward with a torch in his hand. Slocum kept firing even after the man fell dead to the ground. The torch the cowboy had intended for the roof of the Tewksbury house landed on his chest and set fire to his shirt. In a few seconds the man's corpse was ablaze. This caused those with Cooper to jump up to give voice to their fury. Slocum winged two more of them before Cooper urged them to get their heads down.

"That you inside, Slocum?" Cooper shouted. "It's got to be. Who else would shoot a dead man?"

"It wasn't you, Cooper, since he didn't catch the lead in the back." Slocum hoped to flush Cooper with the taunt, but the killer didn't rise to the bait.

"If you surrender, Slocum, I'll let you go. You and ever'one else in there. All we want to do is level the house and barn."

"And steal the horses and cattle."

"You can have the damned sheep."

This produced scattered laughter among Cooper's followers. Slocum waited for another one to poke up his head from hiding, but they had turned cautious now.

"H-he's going to kill us," Lydia said.

"Probably," Slocum allowed, "but the idea is to make him work for it. If he gets careless and I get a good shot, that'll end it. His men don't care squat about the house or even the people in it. Cooper's what's driving them."

"He can starve us out. We don't have much food."

Slocum looked around at the few remaining fighters. They wouldn't need much food if Cooper decided to lay siege to the house, but Slocum knew it would never come to that. Cooper was an impatient man, and not finding Tewksbury here would send him on his way fast, no matter how many of his own men he lost destroying the house.

Slocum opened the door a crack and called out, "If we send Tewksbury out, is that good enough for you to let the rest of us go free?"

"Tewksbury's there?"

"Is it a deal?"

"Slocum, what are you doing? Pa's not here!"

"So? If it buys us a few more minutes, good. We're playing to stay alive, and every second we're not dead, all the better."

"You just want to taunt him."

"That entered my head," Slocum said with a slight grin.

"No deal, Slocum. I want you, too. You and Tewksbury both. Or we'll burn the place down."

"You want to do that, anyway," Slocum called. "Tewksbury's wounded something fierce. He might not last much longer. I reckon you want to kill him yourself."

"And you, Slocum, and you!"

Cooper's patience had run out. He gave the signal for his men to begin their frontal assault. It wasn't a pretty attack or one very well thought out, but it didn't have to be. Other than Slocum and Lydia, no one inside the house was uninjured. As Slocum moved, he felt more than a twinge from the wounds Shotgun Larsen had given him. He was even a tad lightheaded, though that had gone away for a spell after the fine breakfast Mrs. Graham had given him.

Slocum settled down, back against the wall, and thought on her. It was a pity he hadn't come across her earlier, but then it wouldn't have mattered, since she was seeing John Tewksbury and married to Tom Graham. Before he could ponder on who had shot Graham, the wall above him exploded.

"Here they come," Lydia cried.

Cooper and his men rode toward them full tilt, firing as fast as they could.

"Make every shot count," Slocum warned. "They'll be on us in an instant."

He swung his rifle up and fired twice, then frowned. Something was different. The intensity of fire had increased drastically, but it didn't seem to be coming from Cooper and his men. They were twisted around in the saddles, firing over their shoulders—and dying as they did.

"We got help," Slocum shouted. "Give 'em all you got!"

He fired until the magazine came up empty, grabbed a fallen rifle and emptied that, then whipped out his Colt Navy and began firing it. The air took on a fine red mist from the blood of Cooper's men dying. And then there fell an eerie silence, interrupted only by the sporadic moans of wounded men strewn on the ground around the front of the house.

Slocum stepped out onto the porch and saw Tewksbury and twenty or more ranchers trotting up. All held smoking rifles or pistols.

"Took you long enough to get here," Slocum said.

"Had to stop and pay my respects to Mrs. Graham," Tewksbury said, grinning crookedly.

"She tell you what Cooper was planning?"

"That and she said you was gonna hole up here to protect Lydia and the rest. Burnin' down the Blevins place weren't half as much fun as cuttin' down Cooper and his men."

"Where is he?" Slocum stepped out into the mud caused by the tremendous outpouring of blood. He walked around hunting for Andy Cooper but didn't find him. "Anybody get away?"

"Not so's I saw, but then I was blinded by all that gunsmoke. Filled the air, it did, we was firin' so hard."

Slocum listened to Tewksbury go on and on about how

he had chosen to attack Cooper in the same way that Cooper had caught him earlier, but Slocum knew it was all chin music. If Mrs. Graham hadn't happened to tell Tewksbury where Cooper was and what he intended, the rancher would have ridden on to the Blevins spread and a whole passel more would be dead.

Slocum included.

"He's not here. He got away." Slocum wiped the sweat and dirt from his forehead and looked around. The only place Cooper could have gone was to the west. When Tewksbury had attacked, Andy Cooper had kept riding rather than turning to see what was going on. That instinctive cowardice had saved him again.

"Son of a bitch," Slocum said, "he's shot so many men in the back he figures that's what everyone else wants to do to him."

"Cain't say he's far wrong."

"Give me a horse," Slocum said. "I'll track him down."

"He ain't a threat now that we done killed all his boys. The ones what ain't dead are gonna think twice 'bout crossin' John Tewksbury."

Slocum started to tell Tewksbury how wrong that was, as long as Cooper still lived. Most of the man's gang still roamed through the Tonto Basin, maybe even holed up at the Blevins spread waiting to ambush Tewksbury and his men. Nothing would get through to the rancher right now. Slocum grabbed a sturdy horse, swung into the saddle and then caught the reins of another. By switching off, he would always have a fresh mount and eventually overtake Cooper, no matter how hard the man rode away.

He headed out to find Cooper's trail and never looked back when he heard Lydia call his name.

18

Slocum zigzagged back and forth making sure that Cooper didn't suddenly veer away from the path he had taken. Cooper had reacted quickly to Tewksbury's attack, riding due west, but there was no hint that he was turning cagey. He was flat-out running for life. Slocum had to admit Cooper might have been a coward, but he wasn't stupid.

As he rode, Slocum made sure his rifles were loaded. He wished he had taken the time to get more ammunition for his Colt, but it hadn't occurred to him. Catching Cooper had been his only thought, and now such impetuosity might come back to haunt him. He had a pair of rifles, and those would have to do him.

The way he felt, he could take on Cooper with his bare hands and rip the man to shreds. From the spacing of the hoofprints, Slocum saw that Cooper's horse had begun to falter as it worked up one of the rolling hills that dotted the Tonto Basin. Going more slowly, to be sure Cooper wasn't on the ridge waiting to shoot him from ambush, wasted time. Slocum gritted his teeth, braced for a bullet and pressed on as fast as possible. Stopping Cooper was the only thing that mattered. When he reached the summit, he saw Cooper with his horse near a watering hole in the valley beyond. Judging from the lathered flanks and the way it wobbled on its legs, Cooper's horse had run its race.

"Howdy, Cooper," Slocum called, knowing the man wasn't going to race off.

"Slocum!" Cooper's hand flashed for his six-shooter. He drew and fired—or tried to. The hammer fell on an empty cylinder. Seeing he was out of ammo and, like Slocum, had not reloaded his sidearm, Cooper grabbed for the rifle sheathed at his saddle.

Slocum bided his time, drawing his rifle, levering in a fresh cartridge and taking careful aim. Cooper dragged his rifle out and frantically worked the cocking lever. Over and over he worked it. The expression on his face told Slocum the man was out of ammunition. All he had to do was pull back on his trigger and end Cooper's miserable life.

"Walk away from the horse, Cooper," Slocum ordered. He squeezed off a round that kicked up dirt between Cooper's boots to get him moving.

Slocum rode forward slowly and then dismounted, never taking his eyes off Cooper.

"Tables are turned now," Slocum said. "What should I do with you?"

"We don't have any quarrel," Cooper said, licking his lips and looking around like a trapped rabbit wanting to run off and hide. "Me and you, Slocum, we're alike. Two peas in a pod. I remember that the law was lookin' for you. We can work this out."

"You shot my partner back in Texas. Shot him in the back."

"I didn't know he was your partner. Honest." Cooper swallowed hard. "Who was he?"

"Hezekiah Clayton. You don't even know his name. You know the names of the others you shot in the back?"

"You can't gun me down in cold blood, Slocum. You're not the kind." Cooper blanched when he looked into Slocum's eyes and saw the determination of the man he faced.

The sound of a horse approaching caused Slocum to glance away for a split second. This was all the time it took

Cooper to go for a hideout gun in his vest pocket. He got it out and fired, but Slocum was moving fast. The slug went past him and buried itself in a tree trunk. Slocum ended up on his belly on the ground, his rifle pointed directly at Andy Cooper.

"No, no, Slocum. Look, I'm throwin' away the der-ringer. I'm unarmed. You won't shoot an unarmed man in cold blood!"

"You're right," said Slocum, and he got to work.

He stood by the pond, rifle resting in the crook of his arm as Mrs. Graham rode up. Her turquoise eyes flitted from Slocum to Cooper and back. She smiled.

"Glad to find you still breathing," she said. She looked from Slocum to the oak tree behind him. Her eyes widened a little when she fully understood Cooper's predicament. "You've been busy."

Slocum glanced over his shoulder at Cooper astride his exhausted horse. Cooper tried to cry out in fear but couldn't. The noose cinched around his neck tightened every time his horse shifted under him to graze at the lush grass underfoot.

"You going to leave him like that?" the woman asked.

"He should have hung a long time back."

"There's a sheriff from over in Prescott with a posse who showed up at the ranch not an hour ago," Mrs. Graham said. "It was a big posse. The governor has heard about all the trouble in the Basin and sent the sheriff to stop it."

"Reckon losing a deputy was enough to get their atten-tion," Slocum said. "If they want to take Cooper in, they can."

"If he doesn't hang himself?"

"That's right," Slocum said. He climbed into the saddle.

"S-Slocum, don't l-leave me like this," Cooper pleaded. He choked when his horse moved beneath him. The horse eyed the pond and considered what it would be like to swallow some of the clear, cool water after getting its fill of grass. Cooper managed to use his knees to control the horse and keep it from wandering off. This time.

"You're lucky I think so much of horses, Cooper," Slocum said. "Otherwise, I'd set fire to its tail. Now, excuse me, if you will. I've got some cattle to round up and herd out of here."

"You leaving the Basin?" asked Mrs. Graham. "Mind if I ride with you? If you're herding very many cattle, you can use some help."

"You know how?"

"Can't be as hard as some of the things I've done."

"Your husband?" Slocum asked. The woman pushed back the long canvas duster she wore and rested her hand on the butt of a pistol holstered at her hip.

"That wasn't hard at all," she said.

As they rode off together, Slocum said, "I've decided to drive the cattle south where I can get a decent price, maybe to Tucson. There'll be Apaches along the way." Going to Prescott with the law all riled up might not be a good idea. North meant running into what remained of Cooper's gang. And heading east was out of the question. In that direction lay Tewksbury and the sheriff—and Lydia.

"That sounds like a good idea. Things might not be too hot in Tucson, other than the sun," she said. "It's been a lot more dangerous in the Tonto Basin lately."

"It has," Slocum allowed, looking sideways at her. She was a mighty fine-looking woman. "But I've got one question, if we're going to be on the trail together."

"Judith," she said. "My first name's Judith."

Slocum nodded. It was going to be a good ride south.

JAKE LOGAN
TODAY'S HOTTEST ACTION WESTERN!